Praise for *Soul Bonds: Common Powers 1*

"I highly recommend Sammi and Mitchell's passionate, sexy and intense love story. I'm happy to report that Lynn Lorenz's new supernatural series, Common Powers, gets off to a fantastic start with *Soul Bonds*."

— Marame, *Rainbow Reviews*

"*[Soul Bonds]* is a story that is absolutely amazing in theory and is well executed by a superb author. Lynn Lorenz has definitely proven that her writing is at the top of the gay erotic romance category. Definitely a must read story by a must read author."

— Kimberly Spinney, *Ecataromance*

"Ms. Lorenz has blended a contemporary story with a paranormal flare that combines to create a fascinating story."

— Teresa, *Fallen Angel Reviews*

"*Soul Bonds* is another winner for Ms. Lorenz."

— *Literary Nymphs*

Soul Bonds is the first paranormal story in a contemporary setting that I have read from this author... I thought that she did a great job on the characterizations of both Sammi and Mitchell...

— *Jessewave*

LooseId ®

ISBN 10: 1-59632-820-7
ISBN 13: 978-1-59632-820-4
SOUL BONDS: COMMON POWERS 1
Copyright © February 2009 by Lynn Lorenz
Originally released in e-book format in July 2008

Cover Art and Design by April Martinez

DISCLAIMER: Many of the acts described in our BDSM/fetish titles can be dangerous. Please do not try any new sexual practice, whether it be fire, rope, or whip play, without the guidance of an experienced practitioner. Neither Loose Id nor its authors will be responsible for any loss, harm, injury or death resulting from use of the information contained in any of its titles.

This book is an original publication of Loose Id. Each individual story herein was previously published in e-book format only by Loose Id and is a work of fiction. Any similarity to actual persons, events or existing locations is entirely coincidental.

Printed in the U.S.A. by
Lightning Source, Inc.
1246 Heil Quaker Blvd
La Vergne TN 37086
www.lightningsource.com

COMMON POWERS 1:
SOUL BONDS

Lynn Lorenz

Chapter One

Sammi slipped between the shadows of the houses that bordered the avenue. His heart thudded as he pressed his back against the rough brick, and with a quick swipe he pushed back the hair that fell over his eyes. There was no way he was going back to Donovan.

Enough was enough.

With his teeth clenched so tight they ached, Sammi watched for the black Town Car. Donovan and his men would be looking for him again tonight. Sammi didn't know how much longer he could survive on the streets of Houston. For someone with no money, no identity, and no friends, they could be deadly.

The bar was just half a block away.

If he ran, he could be inside before the traffic light at the corner changed. He bent, his lean body coiled to spring from his position, when Donovan's black Lincoln slid around the corner, and like a shark looking for prey, cruised toward him.

With a quick gasp he blocked off his mind and disappeared into the shadows.

The car slowed, pulled to the curb, and stopped in front of the bar.

Sammi exhaled. Three breaths later the passenger door opened. Sammi watched as Donovan's muscle Moretti pried his massive body from the seat and then disappeared inside the nightclub. Moretti would be getting some odd looks, but it wouldn't be the first time the big goon had cruised bars looking for boys for his boss.

Edging closer to the corner of the house, Sammi peeked around it. Moretti had been in there for several minutes. Probably scanning the place. Maybe even barging in on the back rooms to see if Sammi was giving some pick-up head.

Fifteen minutes later, and Moretti would have caught Sammi.

Moretti's timing sucked tonight.

The club's door opened and Moretti exited. With a shake of his cue ball head, he wedged himself back in the car and slammed the door shut. The Town Car pulled away from the curb and headed toward Sammi, hidden in the shadows. Holding his breath, terrified he'd give away his hiding place, he slipped the small folding knife from his pocket and flipped it open. He'd rather die than go back to Donovan.

His only hope for safety lay inside the bar. Once there, he'd open his mind, find a willing partner, and get off the streets for the night.

The car stopped at the light. Sammi let out a slow breath. The light changed and the traffic began moving. With another four deep breaths, he watched as the Town Car disappeared in the heavy traffic of Montrose. He closed the knife with a click and shoved it back into his jeans.

Sammi broke from the shadows and raced to the bar's entry.

* * *

Mitchell sat at the bar and nursed his scotch. All around him, music pulsed and men moved in and out of the shadows. The dance floor seethed with bodies. Couples danced, some with tentative touches and gentle caresses, while others gyrated, their hips in sync with the rhythm of the pounding bass. Still, some danced alone, feeling the freedom of movement and no necessity for a partner.

What the hell am I doing here?

He wasn't going to pick up anyone. Not tonight. Not any night. He'd sworn off the fast life; it was far too dangerous.

Who was he kidding? He was the king of denial.

Crown me.

Mitchell scanned the men.

Even if he saw someone he liked, and he hadn't in a very long time, he wouldn't break his rule and take anyone home. It wasn't safe. There was no telling whom he might bring home. Time was he only worried about serial killers, but these days, he had to deal with gay bashers.

Besides, he really hated that awkward parting in the morning. Should he serve breakfast or just put the guy out? A kiss goodbye, or lie and tell him he'd call?

A quick blowjob in the back rooms of the bar would avoid all that trouble.

If he was looking. And he wasn't.

His gaze raked over several younger men standing at the end of the bar. Tight leather snugged over tight asses, dark liner around their hungry eyes.

He liked younger, but tonight there wasn't a flicker of arousal from between his legs. Not even half-mast, much less fully flying the colors. What was wrong with him? There were some very good-looking men here tonight and if he put forth the effort, he could pick up one of them and head to the back.

He just couldn't stand another empty fuck.

Sammi leaned against the wall of the bar and closed his eyes. Opening his mind, he listened. The music faded away and indistinct voices floated in blackness, pieces of soft conversations, snips of laughter, a few suggestive words, all faint whispers in the night. All he had to do was pick one out, focus on it, and make his move.

What the hell am I doing here?

Sammi jumped as the words shouted in his mind. His eyes flew open and Sammi scanned the darkened room for the man who'd thought them. Like the wicked, sharp blade of his knife, the voice had sliced through all the chatter like butter and set his body quivering and brought his cock to rigid attention.

I'm better off alone.

Effortlessly, he locked onto a man sitting at the bar. It had never been that easy before. Sammi's heart hammered at the chance he'd found him. The one. His soul bond. He shook his head, took a deep breath to quell the excitement, and stared at the man whose voice had risen above all the others, pushing them into nothing more than background noise, mere static on the constant radio that played in Sammi's head.

Long legs clad in faded blue jeans. A white T-shirt peeked from under a brown leather jacket. Loafers, no socks. Dark wavy hair, broad shoulders. Early thirties.

Sammi drew closer, weaved in and out of the gyrating dancers as he crossed the dance floor. Unable, unwilling, to take his eyes off the man.

A young man slid onto the chair next to Mitchell. Male musk enveloped Mitchell, as if the guy were shooting off pheromones meant for him alone. *Nice.*

The bartender walked over. "What can I get you?"

"I'll have what he's drinking and put it on his tab." A soft, yet damned sexy, voice filled Mitchell's ears, shot through his body, and landed in his cock.

He turned to look at the man who'd given him an instant hard-on.

The bartender raised an eyebrow. "That okay?"

"Yeah. It's fine," Mitchell said without taking his eyes off the stranger.

The young man faced him, pushed the long forelock of straight dark hair from his eyes, and their gazes locked. As if he'd leaned too far over the top rail of a skyscraper, Mitchell plummeted into endless dark eyes. Aware of the sudden pounding of his heart and the tightness of his jeans, he swallowed, afraid to speak. Afraid he'd chase away this remarkable creature.

He was the sweetest thing Mitchell had seen in a long time.

"You think I'm the best thing you've seen in a while." He offered a soft smile and placed his hand on Mitchell's thigh. The gentle touch seared him and he caught fire.

"Yeah." Mitchell gave a grunt.

His heat-filled gaze raked over the man. Young, maybe mid-twenties, lean but muscled. Despite the dead sexy mop of bangs that fell over his face, his hair was cut short on the sides and back.

What did Mitchell's rules have to say about this?

Damn, he couldn't recall a single one, but he knew he'd be breaking most of them before the sun rose. "What else am I thinking?"

"That you want to break all your rules with me."

Mitchell's foot slipped off the rung. Almost falling off the chair, he reached for the edge of the bar to hold himself upright. How the hell did this guy know what he was thinking?

"Look, I don't know what game you're playing, but..." Mitchell growled, his body tensing along with his fists.

"No game." He shook his head and the bangs swayed, giving Mitchell a peek at those eyes again. "Are you always such a hard ass?"

Placing his knees between Mitchell's, he leaned closer and laid his smaller hand over Mitchell's tight fist. It relaxed beneath the touch like butter on a summer day. The guy's other hand slid along Mitchell's thigh, trailing fire.

Stopping where thigh met hip, he glanced down between Mitchell's legs. "This is the only thing that should be hard." His thumb brushed over the lump in Mitchell's too-tight jeans.

Mitchell's cock twitched in happy greeting to the hand that touched it, and his balls pulled in so tight he thought they'd disappear. Not in a bad way. But in a way that said oh yeah, this would be a fuck he'd never forget. A fuck he wanted more than anything on earth. More than his next breath. And he wanted it right now.

"Let's go to your place." That voice sent delighted shivers down Mitchell's spine. Damn, he was fucking helpless against it.

"What's your name?" He didn't know what else to say.

"Sammi. What's yours?"

"Mitchell."

"Well, Mitchell," Sammi purred as he slid off the chair and into the space directly in front of Mitchell. Mitchell stood, rising a head taller than Sammi. Looking down into liquid brown eyes, Mitchell grabbed the young man's narrow hips, pulled him to his body, and ground his hard-on against Sammi's belly. "I think we're on the same wavelength," Sammi finished as he tilted his head back and offered his lips.

"Yeah." Mitchell leaned down, took the kiss, and broke his rule about not kissing strange men he met at bars. Soft at first, then as Sammi's tongue flicked against his lips to ask for admittance, Mitchell opened to him. They deepened the kiss.

Damn, Sammi was sinfully delicious, a blend of vanilla and sugar cookies with a chocolate aftertaste. What would his skin taste like? Or his cock? A firestorm erupted inside

Mitchell. He didn't want to wait until he got Sammi home to find out. He'd do him against the bar right now if he could.

This was insane.

He wanted Sammi and Sammi wanted him. That message was coming through to Mitchell loud and clear, as if Sammi had spoken the words. Of all the men the guy could have, and Mitchell knew Sammi could take his pick, he'd picked him. Why was he so damned lucky?

"You're the only man in this place worth a damn," Sammi answered Mitchell's doubts. "Let's get out of here."

"Oh, yeah."

Fuck. There went the rule about bringing strangers home. Mitchell dug into his pocket and tossed a twenty on the bar. Taking Sammi's hand, he led the way to the door, pulled it open, and stepped out, towing Sammi by the hand behind him.

"I live just up the street and around the corner."

Like a dog follows its master, like summer follows spring, Sammi followed Mitchell. If Sammi had had a tail, it would have been wagging. He was definitely panting in anticipation.

Mitchell's voice had captured his heart the first time he'd heard it in his mind, and it had gone straight to his soul. And when he'd touched Mitchell, he'd burned with a desire he'd often faked but had never known.

He'd gone into the bar in hopes of swapping his body for a night's brief protection from the man who owned him, just as he'd done the last five nights. Instead, he'd found his destiny.

Mitchell. The one person who could hear Sammi as well as Sammi heard him. No words would be needed between them, only thoughts and emotions. If they made love, gave themselves to each other, the connection between them would be forged.

Strong. Lasting. Unbreakable.

They hurried through the night. By the time they'd turned the corner, they were running, hand-in-hand, down the street to Mitchell's four-plex.

Flying up the stairs to the second floor apartment, Mitchell slammed into the front door.

"Fuck! My keys." Chest heaving, he dug them out of his pocket, fumbled with the lock, and then pushed the door open.

They fell inside, tumbling together in a lust-driven rush to get to each other's bodies. Mitchell kicked the door shut and stripped off his jacket. Frenzied, two sets of hands pulled on belts, unsnapped buttons, slid zippers down, and jerked jeans open as lips kissed, teeth nipped, and tongues sparred.

Sammi won.

After falling to his knees, he pulled Mitchell's cock free. He wanted Mitchell to fuck him, but first, he wanted Mitchell in his mouth.

Every pleasure zone in Sammi's body tingled at the glorious sight of it, thick and long. Velvet headed, brown sheathed, his heavy balls pulled tight to his body, Mitchell's cock was every fantasy Sammi had ever closed his eyes and jerked off to.

Sammi's tongue laved the engorged head.

"Oh, God!" Mitchell cried out and fell back against the wall, burying his hands in Sammi's hair as Sammi wrapped his hand around the base of Mitchell's prick.

As pleasure poured off Mitchell, Sammi opened himself to it and drank it in. It filled Sammi's cock as he licked, sucked, teased, and taunted Mitchell's magnificent prick and swamped his pleasure centers. Near madness, Sammi gathered Mitchell's pleasure and folded it into his own.

Mitchell held nothing back and Sammi took everything he was given.

"Fuck, I'm coming."

"Not yet." Still on his knees, Sammi ringed the head of Mitchell's cock with his thumb and forefinger and squeezed, cutting off the impending orgasm.

"Shit," Mitchell groaned.

Sammi felt Mitchell's pain, pleasure, and frustration at not coming. Using all his talent, all his experience, all his passion, he'd give Mitchell the best orgasm of his life.

It would rock both of them.

It would bond them together forever.

It would free Sammi from Donovan.

"Fuck me," Sammi begged.

"Oh, yeah," Mitchell rasped.

Sammi's tongue had been doing the most incredible things to Mitchell's cock and having to stop nearly killed him, but the pain was fucking delicious.

Damn, he wanted more of Sammi. He pulled Sammi to his feet and kissed him, driving him across the hall. They thudded against the wall and sent a picture crashing to the floor.

Sammi climbed Mitchell as if he were a mountain, legs wrapped around his waist, arms looped around his shoulders, his smaller body easily held in the larger man's arms.

Still rigid, his cock stood painfully trapped between Sammi's body and his own belly. Raining kisses on Sammi's face, Mitchell carried him down the hall to his bedroom.

Once in the room, Mitchell peeled Sammi from him. "Take off your clothes or I'll rip them off," he growled.

"No, wait! They're the only ones I have," Sammi cried out. He broke away long enough to undress, as Mitchell kicked off his shoes, shucked out of his jeans, and pulled his T-shirt over his head.

He scooped Sammi up, then tossed him on the bed. Sammi rolled and came up on his knees. "I know what you want," he rasped.

"Good." Mitchell climbed onto the bed and pushed Sammie down. Stretching over Sammi as if he were about to do a set of pushups, Mitchell held him suspended in air.

Their eyes locked. Mitchell lowered himself. Skin met skin. Caught and ignited. Heat scorched them. Both men gasped as they felt the flames of their pleasure dance over their skin, raising the fine hairs on both their bodies.

"Do you feel that?" Sammi asked, as his hands stroked over Mitchell's back.

Mitchell pulled Sammi over on top of him. "Oh, God, yeah. Like nothing I've ever felt." Mitchell's hands cupped Sammi's firm ass and pulled it against him. Sammi's cock ground into Mitchell's belly.

"This is how it could be forever, with us," Sammi whispered.

"It's so good." And it was. Better than anything Mitchell had ever felt, or dreamed of feeling. How could it be? So fast, so soon? What the hell was happening?

"It gets better."

Sammi wrapped his arms around Mitchell and rolled over, bringing Mitchell back on top. His legs spread open, and Mitchell's hips and legs fell in between them. Pushing up on one arm as he reached down, Mitchell guided his straining cock to Sammi's sweet opening, then froze.

"Fuck, no lube and no condoms." Mitchell rolled to the side, yanked open the nightstand drawer, snatched up the bottle of lube, and tossed it on the bed. His hand scrambled in the drawer searching for a condom.

"Fuck," he swore when his hand came up empty.

"Forget it. Just use the lube and fuck me." Sammi's voice wavered.

Mitchell was on the edge of breaking the gay man's golden rule. It was insane. It was playing with death. He was clean, but Sammi? Wracking his brain, he remembered seeing some in the bathroom.

"No, wait," he gasped as he lurched off the bed and into the bathroom. After searching the second drawer he opened, he found the condoms. He rushed back into the room with the box raised as if he'd discovered something marvelous and precious, then jumped back into bed.

Kneeling beside Sammi, he watched as Sammi pumped his beautiful cock with one hand and stroked the skin behind his balls with the fingertips of the other. Sammi's pubic hair had been trimmed short into a neat dark patch, and his balls were smooth, free of any hair.

Damn, it turned Mitchell on.

"You like watching me touch myself, don't you?" Sammi purred. Squeezing a dab of lube onto his fingertips, he reached lower and bathed his tunnel with it. Slipping a finger into his own backdoor, Sammi groaned, his eyes never leaving Mitchell's.

Mitchell groaned back. "Yeah." Could his cock get any harder? As Sammi's finger slipped in and out of his own ass, he had a fuck-me look on his face, eyes slitted, lips parted, his pink tongue just visible, that drove Mitchell wild.

Unable to stand it another second, Mitchell ripped open the condom, rolled it on, and leaned forward. "Take your finger out, Sammi. I have something better to fuck you with."

"Oh God, yes." Sammi pulled out his finger.

Mitchell caught Sammi's knee in the crook of his arm, leaned forward, and opened him wider. He found Sammi's tight portal, pressed the head of his cock against it, and sank in. Both men cried out as Mitchell filled Sammi.

Mitchell's body covered Sammi as he shuddered beneath him, and it reverberated through both of them. They hung onto the edge of a cliff, eternity stretching out before them.

Mitchell began to pump.

He couldn't take his eyes off Sammi as his lean, sculpted body writhed on the bed, the sheets fisted in his hands. Damn, he was achingly beautiful in the throes of pleasure, yet with a vulnerability that tore into Mitchell's heart.

Sammi's chest was well-defined and smooth, his belly rippled as if he'd spent time in the gym. Two dark, small, rigid nipples tempted Mitchell, and that wild forelock of dark hair fell over Sammi's face, cloaking his eyes. His full lips parted as he panted and his pink tongue darted out to moisten them in a slow swipe.

Everything about Sammi drove Mitchell insane with desire and lust, as if this creature had been created solely for Mitchell's pleasure.

As Mitchell pounded into him, Sammi's body rocked with each thrust. Wrapped in the hot velvet of Sammi's tight tunnel, Mitchell's cock stroked in and out, sending pleasure shooting straight to Mitchell's balls.

Lost in a haze of arousal, Mitchell experienced both their pleasures, as if he could feel what Sammi felt as well as his own pleasure.

"Do you feel that? It's wild," Mitchell gasped.

"Oh God, yes, it's so good. This is it, Mitch. This is you and me together. You belong to me and I belong to you. Can't you feel it?" Sammi cried out, his hands clutching Mitchell's shoulders.

"Shit. This is crazy." He'd just met Sammi, he didn't even know him. Mitch shook his head. Had he lost his mind?

"None of that matters. Only this." *Only us.*

Mitchell held Sammi's hips and thrust harder and deeper as if he wanted to bury himself inside Sammi and never come out. *Yeah, only us.*

Sammi keened deep in his throat as Mitch fucked him, then gasped, "Say it. You're mine. You belong to me and I belong to you."

"I belong to you," Mitch conceded as he closed his eyes and let all their combined feelings fill him up, pushing him to the brink of coming. "You are mine," he growled, his fingers digging into Sammi's flesh as he slammed into Sammi's ass like a pile driver.

Mitchell lost reason. Lost all sense, and in that moment, broke his ultimate rule.

He fell in love.

Together, they rode a tidal wave that swelled, built momentum, climbed upward, higher than either of them had ever been before. Poised on the crest of that sweet wave, they opened their eyes and locked gazes.

This was it, the moment Sammi had waited, dreamed, hoped for.

The bonding.

He opened his soul and stripped his heart bare as he poured his love into Mitchell. A vortex of emotion whirled around them like a tornado, sweeping the lovers up in its maelstrom.

Burying his hands in Mitch's hair, Sammi pulled him down into a soul-searing kiss. Eyes open, they clung to each other as if their lives depended on it.

From this point on, their lives would be entwined.

Building in intensity, their bodies seemed to melt into each other and their hearts beat in perfect syncopation. Sammi's breath was Mitchell's breath. They rode the rising crest of a mutual orgasm that promised to open a new world for both of them.

With a final surge, the tidal wave broke over them and they shattered on the rocks.

Chapter Two

The alarm went off. Mitchell awoke, rolled over, and reached for Sammi, but the bed was cold and empty.

Shit. He'd left.

Mitchell's heart stopped. Then as if it had been jump-started, it thudded hard and fast in his chest. Bolting upright, he looked around the room. Sammi's clothes were gone and so were his.

Mitchell had been so naïve to think that after their amazing night together Sammi wouldn't leave. He closed his eyes, fell back on the bed, and sighed.

Sammi.

Mitchell.

Mitchell's eyes flew open and he gave a half-laugh of relief as he ran his hand over his face. Sammi had stayed, not run away, not left him. And in a way Mitchell couldn't understand, they were still connected, even beyond the incredible sex of last night. Last night? Fuck, it had been the most incredible sex of his life.

As he lay in bed, he could still smell Sammi, could smell their lovemaking caught up in the sheets of his bed, and his prick began a slow, steady rise. Mitchell reached down and stroked it, dwelling on thoughts of his lover's amazing body.

The alarm rang again, warning him that this time, he really needed to get his ass out of bed. He slapped it off. Shit. He had to go to work today. He'd rather stay home and make love to Sammi all day, but he had responsibilities and a bastard of a boss who was just looking for a reason to fire him.

The bedroom door opened and Sammi entered, carrying a tray. He wore only a pair of black boxer briefs. Mitchell groaned, recognizing them as a pair of his. Sammi looked better in them than he did. They snugged just right, cupping Sammi's package and emphasizing the muscles of his thighs.

"You like me in these?"

"Yeah. You can wear my briefs anytime."

Sammi grinned and held out the tray. "I made breakfast. I hope you don't mind." He placed the tray on the side table and sat on the bed. He stroked Mitchell's leg as it stuck out of the covers and his fingers played in the dark hairs that covered Mitchell's calf.

"Are you kidding? Breakfast in bed. It doesn't get any better." Mitchell grinned and, along with Sammi, took a piece of bacon and ate. "How long have you been up?"

"For a while. I watched you sleep for about thirty minutes. You know you have this soft snore?"

"Do not." Mitchell grimaced.

"Do too. It's cute." Sammi looked at him from under his bangs.

"I do not snore 'cute'." Mitchell managed to look insulted.

"Do too."

"Do not. What did you do after that?"

"I fixed breakfast and used your washer and dryer. My clothes were beginning to smell." He wrinkled his nose. "They're in the dryer. I hope that's okay."

"It's fine." Mitchell reached for Sammi. "Come here, babe."

Sammi slid into his arms. They kissed. Sammi tasted of bacon with an underlying sweetness. Mitchell's cock stiffened against his thigh. He broke the kiss and sat back.

"I have to go to work. In fact, if I don't get going, I'll be late."

"Can't you stay home?" Sammi pouted, his bottom lip pushed out.

Mitchell wanted to nibble it, it looked so sexy. "No, not today. I have to do the monthly production reports."

Sammi took another piece of bacon. "What do you do?"

"I work for a small oil company downtown. I'm in the commercial division and we handle all the produced oil and gas, estimate how much and what it costs."

"Sounds like a good job. Lots of numbers?" Sammi made a face.

"Yeah, lots of numbers."

"Did you go to college?" Sammi looked almost wistful.

"I have a BBA in business from the University of Texas at Austin."

"Wow. You must be very smart." Sammi stared at Mitchell's leg as he petted it.

"No, just persistent." Mitchell shrugged. "Look, I don't care if you didn't go to college, babe."

"I never finished high school." From under his mop of bangs, Sammi's eyes caught Mitchell's, looking for reassurance.

"I told you, I don't care. What happened? Do you want to tell me?"

"I was in foster care. Moved around a lot. I ran away when I was sixteen and I've been on my own since then."

"Sounds like a rough time." Mitchell reached out and cupped Sammi's chin. "No more rough times, babe."

Sammi smiled and his face lit up. He leaned in to kiss Mitchell. Soft, full lips pillowed Mitchell's mouth. Damn, he wanted Sammi, but there was work.

"I have to go." Mitchell sighed against Sammi's kiss.

"I know."

Mitchell got out of bed and padded to the bathroom. "Listen, I have extra toothbrushes and stuff. Help yourself to whatever you need."

"Okay. Thanks." Sammi crawled back into the bed as Mitchell started the shower.

Fifteen minutes later, Mitchell came out of the bathroom, clean and shaved, and began to dress.

"You want to help me pick out something?" Mitchell stood in the walk-in closet and pointed to his clothing.

Sammi's eyes widened and he shook his head. "I'm not good at that."

Mitchell shrugged. He slipped on a pair of charcoal grey dress slacks and a soft grey dress shirt.

"Which tie?" He held up two ties for Sammi to pick out.

"The blue one." Sammi pointed to the left one.

"Blue it is." Mitchell tossed the loser back into the closet, and the winning tie over his head. Coming back into the room, he began to tie it.

"Let me." Sammi got out of bed and came to him. He concentrated on knotting the tie, then adjusted it and stepped back. "You look handsome."

Mitchell laughed. "Glad you think so. I have to dress up every day, but I'd rather wear jeans." He slipped on his shoes and headed to the door.

Okay, here was the part he hated. Mitchell didn't want Sammi to leave this morning, maybe not ever. But should he ask him to stay, just expect him to be here at the end of the day or tell him he was free to go? It hadn't sounded as if Sammi had anywhere to go.

"I'll be here when you get back," Sammi answered his unspoken question.

"Good." Mitchell stood with his hand on the doorknob. "I'll return at six."

"If someone phones, should I answer it?" Sammi asked.

"Sure. Just take a message or tell them to call back after six."

"What should I say if they ask who I am?" Sammi's questioning dark eyes locked with his.

Mitchell slipped his hand around Sammi's neck, tilted his head up, and ran his thumb along Sammi's jaw. "Tell them you're my lover and that you're staying with me." Mitchell's mouth took Sammi's in a heated kiss. Sammi's body melted against him, and his purr of pleasure rumbled through Mitchell's body.

They were on the verge of igniting, and if that happened Mitchell was going to fuck Sammi right here against the wall. His cock stiffened as he pulled Sammi to him with his other hand.

"God, I want you," he growled. "Fuck work."

"No, go. You need to. Go." Sammi pushed away and opened the door.

Mitchell grinned and gave Sammi's firm ass a gentle slap on his way out. "I'll call you later. Make yourself at home, babe."

"Okay."

* * *

Mitchell rubbed his eyes and refocused on the spreadsheet. He'd arrived thirty minutes late, and as he'd walked to his cube, James White, his boss, had noted it with a raised eyebrow. Mitchell was convinced the man suspected Mitchell was gay. Despite all the corporation's stands on diversity, Mitchell believed James was homophobic.

The rest of the day seemed to drag past and now, after lunch, Mitchell needed a break. He slipped on his hands-free headset and dialed home.

"Hello." Sammi's sexy voice shot through Mitchell like an arrow.

"Hi, babe." Mitchell purred soft and low. Cubicles offered little privacy and he did not intend to let James or anyone else know about his private life.

"I miss you," Sammi said, a sexy pout in his voice.

"Me, too."

"What are you doing?"

"Working on a spreadsheet."

"Numbers?"

"Yeah," he said with a chuckle, "Numbers. What are you doing?"

"Right now, I'm sitting in your recliner." Sammi's voice dropped lower. "I can smell your scent, Mitchell. It's so strong here. Delicious."

"Really?"

"Um-hmm. I'm still wearing your black briefs, but they're very tight."

"How come?" Mitchell licked his lips and hoped Sammi would tell him in detail.

"Because my cock is hard as a rock, just talking to you."

"Take them off," Mitchell whispered and waited for Sammi to speak.

"They're gone. It's just my skin against your leather chair. Feels fantastic. Cool on my ass at first, but it's warming up."

"Yeah. I can't talk much, you know."

"That's okay. I'll talk, you listen."

"Okay." Mitchell's cock was a long, thick rod that throbbed and strained against his pants.

"I'm cupping my balls. You like them, I can tell. So smooth and firm."

Mitchell made a small noise in his throat.

"Would you let me make yours just as smooth?"

"How do you do that?"

"Hot wax. First, I would spread your legs wide and trim your pubes short, like mine. While the wax was warming, I'd suck your balls to make them tight and firm. That helps. Then, when the wax was just right, I'd brush it on with my fingers."

Mitchell's hand dropped to his lap and rubbed against his cock. The thought of Sammi sucking him and then applying the wax with his fingers only made him harder.

"I'd place the sheets over them and then...rrriipp," Sammi growled.

Mitchell's hand kept a steady rhythm as it rubbed along his shaft. Damn, he wanted to hurt, to feel just that right amount of pain mixed with pleasure. It was something he hadn't shared with any of his former lovers. It took a lot of trust to allow someone to hurt you just right and he'd never trusted the others enough.

"Doesn't that hurt?" Mitchell asked. He might never understand how Sammi knew him, what he was thinking, or what he liked; he only knew he'd never had a lover like him. Mitchell couldn't imagine anyone else even coming close to Sammi.

"So fucking bad you think you're going to cry. But, so good, you know, Mitch? Will you let me hurt you, just a little? I know you want me to."

"Yeah, I want you to." Mitchell's eyes shuttered.

"Then, to soothe your aching balls, I'm going to massage oil into them with my tongue. My finger is going to rub the skin beneath your balls, moving closer to your backdoor." Sammi sighed.

"Mmm," Mitchell purred.

"Unbuckle your pants. I want you to touch yourself."

"I'm not sure that would be wise."

"Can anyone see you?"

"Not unless they come into my cube."

"Then do it. Are you behind a desk?"

"Yeah."

"Do it," Sammi urged. "For me."

Mitchell slipped his belt open, popped the button on his pants, and then eased his zipper down just enough for his fingers to touch the head of his cock. "Okay."

"Good. So, my finger is rubbing you, and I move it lower, circling your hole. I can feel where it's all puckered and tight, so I press harder, making you ache for it. You ache for it, don't you?" he breathed.

"Yeah." Mitchell's fingers ran along the ridge of his head, rough friction against it making his balls tighten.

"Then, I'm going to slip my finger inside you. Plunge it in, no lube. Just my finger reaming your ass," Sammi gasped. "I'm going to rub your sweet spot until you explode."

Mitchell swallowed his groan but couldn't stop the shudder that shot through him. He wanted to know if Sammi was touching himself. "What are you doing?"

"I'm stroking my prick, hard and fast. I'm using a little lube, you know, so it glides, but I still get a little skin-on-skin friction. Do you know what I mean?"

"Yeah, I know. That's good."

"My balls are tight and I'm almost ready to pop."

"What are you doing?"

"Squeezing them, pulling them up so I can reach the skin under them. What are you doing now?"

"Rubbing the head."

"I wish I were there, kneeling between your legs, tucked under your desk."

"What would you do?"

"Oh, I'd suck you until you came. You'd come so hard you'd have to bite a pencil to keep from screaming."

Mitchell groaned softly. "I can't stand this."

"Then come. Come for me, for your Sammi."

Mitchell's hand squeezed and his zipper slid farther down. He pushed his hips forward to give himself room and a better grip on his prick. He jerked open a drawer, pulled out a napkin to shoot into, and like a piston, kept pumping with one hand.

"Are you coming?" Sammi asked breathlessly. "I'm almost there, Mitch."

"Yeah." Mitchell closed his eyes, lost in the vision of Sammi stretched naked on the leather recliner, stroking himself, his glorious cock full and blood engorged, just ripe and ready to explode.

"Oh, God, Mitch. You make me cream like a bitch. Here it comes. Oh baby, yes I'm coming for you Mitch...fuck, here it...oh God." Sammi's cry sounded strangled as he came.

Mitchell came right after Sammi's last gasp. Clamping his lips shut, Mitchell shot his load into the napkin. Shudders ran through his body as each wave of pleasure crashed over him.

"What the hell are you doing?"

Mitchell's eyes flew open and he twisted in his chair. Standing behind him was James, his face in a grimace of disgust. Fuck, how was he going to get out of this? Maybe his boss hadn't known what was going on.

Mitchell pushed his cock down and out of sight. "Nothing."

James placed his arms on the back of Mitchell's chair and leaned over to speak in Mitchell's ear. "See me in my office as soon as you've zipped up." Then, he was gone.

"Mitch? Who was that?" Sammi's voice wavered.

"My boss. Got to go." He hung up.

Crap, this was it. James would fire him, no doubt about that. Son of a bitch. How fucking stupid had that been? He'd lost his mind doing that stunt. Ten years into the company and his career had just slid down the toilet, slick as shit.

Maybe he could do some damage control.

Maybe James would understand about a new lover. He was a man, after all.

Maybe monkeys could fly out his ass.

Mitchell arranged himself, zipped up, and rolled his chair back. Then, he removed his headset, stood, and went to face his fate.

"Close the door and sit down, Mitchell." James motioned to the chair in front of his desk.

Mitchell sat and rested his hands on the arms of the chair. He waited for James to talk first; no point in jumping in until he saw how it would go down.

James leaned back in his large leather executive chair and stared at Mitchell. His blue eyes glinted in what Mitchell could only guess was anticipation of the kill. The silence stretched as each man waited for the other to speak.

James broke first. "Just what did you think you were doing, jerking off in your cube?"

"I know. It was incredibly stupid."

"What was going through your head?

"Obviously not much." Mitchell grimaced. "Truthfully, I have this hot new lover and…" Mitchell shrugged. "You remember how it was." James was married, with kids.

"Yes, I do. Nevertheless, that doesn't excuse what you did. What if one of the women in the department had come by and seen that?"

"I know." His only recourse was to be contrite and throw himself at James's mercy. "I'm very sorry. It won't happen again."

"No, it won't. I'm going to have to send this on to H.R., Mitchell. Because of what you are, this has to be handled through proper channels. If it were up to me, I'd fire you right now."

"What do you mean, 'what I am?'" Mitchell's hackles rose. He knew just where James was going with this.

"Mitchell, let's be honest. I've suspected for some time you were gay. All the signs were there."

"Suspected? All the signs?" Was it a crime? Did James have gaydar?

"No wife, no girlfriends, no pictures on your desk." James shrugged as if that was enough to convict.

"There are lots of unmarried men in this department. What does that have to do with anything? And even *if* I *were* gay, it's no one's business. That's the company policy." Thank God, most major corporations were heavy into diversity and inclusion. Still, that wouldn't dismiss what he'd done, gay or not, and Mitchell knew it.

"And it's because of company policy that I'm giving you a break. I'm going to let H.R. handle this. But, for now, why don't you take the rest of the day off. When you come in tomorrow, we'll see what they have to say about it. If you're lucky, it will just go down in your file and not lead to a dismissal."

"Right. Thanks, James." Mitchell stood. James had cut him more slack than he'd expected.

Mitchell left the office and returned to his cubicle. He saved his worksheet, shut down his computer, and locked his cabinets. As he headed for the elevator, he couldn't figure out what had come over him. Had he lost his mind?

His desire for his lover had blinded him to common sense and decorum, placing his entire career in jeopardy. He'd known it was wrong, but in a moment of weakness, he'd allowed Sammi to talk him into it. It was Mitchell's own fault, plain and simple.

In less than twenty-four hours, Sammi had come into his life like a tornado of passion and sex, and had blown Mitchell away, along with his good sense and most of the rules he'd lived his life by.

If he were a stronger man, he'd put Sammi out of his life, but just the thought of living without Sammi made Mitchell's stomach hurt as if someone had driven their fist into it.

Oh God, he had it so bad. The question was, what did he intend to do about it?

Chapter Three

Sammi paced and bit his thumbnail. This was bad. Oh God, he'd gotten Mitchell into trouble, maybe even fired. Shit. He hadn't meant any harm. He'd just been so turned on by Mitchell's voice over the phone that it'd had him rigid and needing release.

He should have taken a cold shower.

He should have just jerked off.

What was Mitchell going to do when he got home? Fear cramped his belly at what Donovan would have done if Sammi had still been at the penthouse and pulled a stunt like that. Pain might be a game for some, but for Donovan it was an art form.

What would it be like to feel Mitchell's wrath?

Sammi wrapped his arms around his body and started to shake. He tried to stop, get control, but the waves of fear shook him. This terror was worse than all the times at Donovan's penthouse. Knees knocking, he struggled to make it to the couch and collapse.

If Mitchell put him out, cast him aside, where would he go? It wouldn't matter where he went, because he wouldn't live long separated from his soul bond.

The key scratched in the lock, the front door opened, and Mitchell walked into the room. Their eyes met. Sammi sucked in his breath, and reached for control. The shakes increased and the building terror overwhelmed him.

"I'm so sorry. I swear it will never happen again. Please." Sammi lurched toward Mitchell. "Don't hurt me. Don't throw me out." He clutched Mitchell's hands as he begged him.

Mitchell didn't push him away or strike him. Without a word, Mitchell gathered Sammi into his arms and held him. Sammi felt Mitchell's lips play against his temple. Mitchell's hand brushed aside Sammi's bangs, tilting his head upward.

"Shhh," Mitchell crooned.

Mitchell kissed him.

Dear God, how could he do that after what Sammi had done? It was so tender, so filled with love. Sammi opened his soul and pulled in Mitchell's emotions, letting them wash over him. Calming him. Reassuring him.

"I love you. Nothing will change that."

"I love you. I'm so sorry."

"It's all right. I just have to talk to H.R. tomorrow morning." Mitchell smiled at him. "Come on, it's fine. Really."

"Are you sure?" Sammi asked.

"Sure."

Mitchell was lying. Sammi could feel his concern and worry. "You can't lie to me, remember?"

"Right. Look, whatever happens tomorrow will happen for a reason. Let's deal with it when it does. Okay?" Mitchell cupped Sammi's chin, raised it, and gazed into his eyes.

"Okay." Sammi gave him a tentative smile, then slid back into Mitchell's arms.

Mitchell led him to the recliner, sat, and pulled him into his lap. Sammi's body tucked perfectly into the bends of Mitchell's body as if they were two halves of a whole.

"Did you really think I'd hurt you?" Mitchell asked as he cupped Sammi's face with the palm of his hand.

"I wasn't sure."

"Has someone hurt you?" Mitchell's voice drew him out.

"Yes. This guy I was with. He used to…beat me if I screwed up." To say Donovan had beaten him was wrong. A beating was simple, straightforward; you took your licks and it was over. Sammi had been beaten in all of his foster homes.

Until he'd met Donovan, Sammi had never known real evil. Those other people were only mean and petty. Donovan was on his own level, a true virtuoso. He used torture, but it was the kind that didn't leave marks on your body. Bodies were important; Donovan's customers paid for beautiful bodies. Donovan had fucked with Sammi's head, made him wonder if he was dead or alive, if it was night or day, or how many days had passed since he'd been fed or had water.

Made Sammi wish he were dead.

In the closet.

In the blackness.

No lights, no sounds.

Sammi began shaking. Mitchell jerked back as images filled his mind.

"It was dark where you were. Small and quiet," Mitchell whispered, his voice trembling. "Shit, Sammi."

"Yes. In the closet." He sighed.

"This guy used to lock you in a closet?" Mitchell growled. "The son of a bitch."

Sammi nodded.

Mitchell pulled him closer. "Is that why you didn't want to pick out my clothes?"

"Yes, they were in the closet."

"Don't worry. That closet doesn't have a lock, babe."

They sat huddled together until Sammi stopped shaking and his breathing went back to normal.

"Sorry. I don't usually break down like that. I'm a grown man, for God's sake." He shook his head and gave a half-hearted laugh.

"Everyone has fears, Sammi. Even me."

"You? What fears do you have?" Sammi leaned up and stared into Mitchell's eyes.

"Well, for one thing, I'm terrified that I might lose you." Mitchell smiled.

Sammi cocked his head to the side. "You are," he gasped. "Don't be, Mitch. I love you so much; I'm never going to leave you." Sammi could no more leave Mitch than Mitch could leave him. They were soul bonded.

"Good. Makes me feel better." He gave Sammi a quick kiss. "Now, let's go get some dinner."

"Dinner?" Sammi frowned. Mitchell wanted to go out, but it was still too soon since Sammi's escape. He was far too valuable for Donovan just to forget about.

"Yes, dinner. That's where you and I go to a restaurant and eat food." Mitchell chuckled.

"How about we order pizza? I'd rather spend the time with you alone." Sammi gave him a wicked smile.

Mitchell's eyebrows rose. "Pizza it is."

* * *

Mitchell's fingers tingled as Sammi licked the last of the pizza sauce from them.

"That was better than going out, wasn't it?" Sammi asked.

"Maybe." Mitchell pulled Sammi close. "Now, time for dessert." He licked Sammi's lips with the tip of his tongue.

Sammi moaned and parted his lips. Mitchell thrust inside. Sammi tasted of garlic, pepperoni, and that odd sweetness. Damn, every time he tasted Sammi it was more delicious than the last. He was addicted. A junkie for sin, sex, and Sammi.

Mitchell's hands clasped Sammi's firm, tight ass and his cock stiffened as he pulled Sammi closer. He wanted to pound Sammi from behind.

"I want to fuck you, babe," he groaned.

"You want me on my knees. On the couch." Sammi stood, pulled his shirt over his head, and took off his pants. Mitchell rose to his feet, undressed, and stood behind him. Looking over Sammi's shoulder, Mitchell wrapped his arms around Sammi and found his cock, already at attention. Sammi's thick flesh felt so good in Mitchell's hand.

"God, babe, I love your cock." He stroked it slowly, from the base upward. His fingers squeezed the very end, coaxing a pearl from its tip. He nibbled on Sammi's neck as he thumbed the droplet over the velvet head of Sammi's cock.

Sammi's head fell back, exposing his throat and his swath of bangs fell to the side, revealing his eyes. They shuttered with pleasure as he moaned. Mitchell opened himself to Sammi's pleasure and it raced through him.

"How the hell do we do that?" Mitchell gasped. Knees bent, his cock nestled in the cleft between Sammi's globes as he rubbed it up and down. As he gave himself pleasure, he knew Sammi felt it also.

"Because we're soul mates."

"Soul mates. Right." If this was what that meant, Mitchell knew he'd never had one before. Sammi was the man meant for him and he was meant for Sammi.

"On your knees," Mitchell ordered.

Sammi knelt on the couch, leaned over the back of it, and pushed his ass into the air. "Fuck me, Mitch."

Mitchell stood behind Sammi as his hands roved over Sammi's body, feeling the muscles in his lower back, the tautness of Sammi's buttocks, the velvet softness of his valley. His fingers stroked the sensitive skin from Sammi's tunnel to his balls, and Sammi shivered with delight.

"You know what I want," Sammi crooned.

"I know what you want." And he did. Mitchell knew what Sammi wanted as if they were his own desires. Mitchell pressed his cock against Sammi's entry, tight, puckered, and pink. "But, first I want to lick you." He bent over and kissed Sammi's hip, working his way with nips and licks to the furrow between Sammi's globes. He'd never rimmed anyone before, but now he longed to flick his tongue against Sammi's sweet rose. Sammi cried out as Mitchell's tongue danced across it. Both men felt the rise of their arousal, of sensual feelings so encompassing that the lovers became lost in each other.

"I want you now." Mitchell tore open a condom and slipped it on. He paused to spread the lube over Sammi and then pressed in. Sammi's backdoor opened for Mitchell as if he had a key.

"Oh God, it's good," Sammi gasped. He arched his back to make it easier for Mitchell to fuck him deeper.

"That's right. So fucking good," Mitchell muttered, his hands gripping tighter as he moved in and out, delving deeper with each stroke. Letting go, his body took over and he no longer concentrated on his hips moving or keeping his balance.

Mitchell, lost in primal lust, in the fuck, hammered Sammi's ass. The cries and whimpers Sammi made, in the sounds of their flesh meeting, of their balls slapping together, and the taste of the salty sweat on his upper lip as he worked to bring them both to orgasm, drove Mitchell on.

Mitchell watched as his cock slid in and out of that marvelous, tight, velvet tunnel. Damn, he loved watching; it was so fucking erotic. His balls tightened and he felt the pressure building. In a few moments, he'd feel the surge fight against the wall and then the sweetness of that wall as it crumbled.

"Harder, Mitch!"

Harder, it was. Mitchell leaned over Sammi's body, pounding in a frenzy, his hips moving like a dynamo, as if he were powered by the electricity that flew between them.

"Oh God, babe, here it comes. Take it. Take my load." Mitchell was relentless as he fucked Sammi and Sammi met every ramming thrust with a thrust of his own, taking Mitchell deep inside him.

"Give it to me…fuck me now…oh shit I'm coming," Sammi shouted.

Mitchell exploded and took Sammi with him over the wall. They merged, falling in an endless tumble, as stars exploded behind their eyelids and their bodies quaked until they collapsed.

Sammi lay beneath Mitchell on the floor. Mitchell gathered him into his arms and nuzzled his lover's neck. Neither one of them were capable of speech or of standing. His chest heaving, Mitchell reached up, pulled the knit throw off the arm of the couch, and wrapped it around them like a cocoon.

Mitchell was lost.

Sammi had come into his life like a tornado, that was true, but the fire that burned in his heart for Sammi was something he knew he couldn't douse.

He'd deal with work in the morning. He could always find another job, but a man like Sammi was a rarity. A precious jewel in a crazy world.

A jewel he had to possess.

* * *

Donovan glared at Moretti. "What do you mean you can't find him?"

"I've been all over the Montrose, boss. Last time he was spotted was four nights ago. The fag who took him home said he was gone before he woke up in the morning."

"What makes you think he's still in Montrose?"

"Easy pickings. Lots of possible marks." Moretti shrugged. "If he leaves the gay district, it's going to be hard for him to find shelter with anyone. But, once lost in the city, he could be one face in four million and we might never get him back."

That was not what Donovan wanted to hear. He hated being told he couldn't have what he wanted, and he wanted Sammi. That young man was worth his weight in gold and that's just what Donovan had planned to charge for him.

The intermediary from Rome had a very special buyer, someone very highly placed. Donovan never asked who the buyers were and he didn't really care as long as they paid, but this time, he suspected the order for a very special young man had come from Vatican City. Still, it could be anyone.

Sammi was the most gifted sex slave Donovan had ever owned, and he'd sparked a bidding war that resulted in the largest bid Donovan had ever seen.

"You have to find him before he leaves Montrose." Donovan closed his eyes and reached out, searching for that small, soft voice in the darkness, but there was nothing.

When he'd first found Sammi and discovered his ability to hear his lover's thoughts, he'd tried to forge a link with the kid, but it had been fragile at best.

Too many visits to the closet had shattered their connection and had nearly destroyed Sammi. Donovan admitted to himself that he'd been foolish, reckless even, to push his prize so hard. But, Sammi had been rebellious, and needed to be taught to mind his master. Seemed it hadn't worked. Sammi had escaped the penthouse and Donovan's guards.

"I've had my men out every night," Moretti said. "No luck so far."

"This time, lose the Town Car. You can see that thing coming from blocks away. Take the new Mercedes; it blends better. Do the bars again, and the tattoo shops, the head shops, have your men check anywhere he might have gone. Try the all-night diners. I want every stone turned over."

Moretti nodded. "Every stone. Right." He lumbered to the door of the penthouse, gave the guard there a nod, and exited.

Donovan walked into his study, to his desk, and sat. He turned on his computer, opened the folder marked "Horses" and searched his stable. There was an order for a blonde girl, a Britney look-a-like, for an Arab prince.

Twelve photos filled the screen. He found two girls in his possession that could work. Donovan closed the other photos and stared at the two left. He'd have his stylist work on Kathy's hair, get it just the right shade. Shauna needed a nose job. That would cost. However, with the amount the prince was paying, it would be nothing. Donovan's reputation as the go-to man would remain intact and his rep was like money in the bank.

Just to be sure, he'd prepare both of the girls. No matter which one he sold to the Arab, he'd sell the other soon enough. Blondes were popular. He emailed his contacts and made all the arrangements.

There was a new message from Rome.

He opened it and read it through, then deleted it.

Fuck. He needed Sammi and fast. If he wasn't found by the end of the week, the deal would be off and the half-million-dollar fee would slip through his fingers. His thin lips grew even thinner.

No matter. If Rome wouldn't take Sammi, there were the losing high bidders who'd love a second chance. Money could still be made.

Donovan swore whoever had been hiding his property was going to regret that he'd ever laid eyes on Sammi.

Chapter Four

Mitchell sat across from the H.R. representative, Ms. Jane Walker, and gave her a tentative smile. She did not smile back.

"Mr. Collins, I've read your supervisor's report." She tapped a folder on her desk with her finger. "It's most...disturbing."

He didn't speak. After ten years in the corporate world, he knew enough to keep his mouth shut, don't admit or deny anything, and let the others dig their own holes. Much safer that way.

Ms. Walker's mouth twisted. "Do you do this all the time?"

"Do what?" Okay, if she was so uptight she couldn't even say the word "masturbate," he was sure she'd never ask if he was homosexual.

"What you were caught doing."

"And that was?" Mitchell raised his eyebrow. Maybe her reluctance to say what he'd done would get him out of this. His hopes rose.

Her mouth quirked and he could see her tongue rolling around behind her thin cheeks as if she had a bad taste in her mouth. "Masturbating," she whispered.

Well, she could say the word after all. Brave girl.

"What was the original question?"

"Do you do that all the time?"

"That depends."

"On what?" She leaned forward in her chair.

"If you mean at home or at work." He really should stop being a smart ass; he was going to get into more trouble, if that was possible.

"At work. What you do at home is none of our business. However, your recent lack of judgment *is* our business." She gave him a stare any grammar school teacher would have been proud to give.

She was right. He'd really screwed up. He waited for her to go on, but this time she waited for his answer. She won.

"I'm really sorry. I don't know what came over me. It won't happen again."

"Well," she huffed, "something had to have spurred this display."

"I have a new lover," Mitchell went with honesty. "We were speaking on the phone and one thing led to another and before I knew it..." He gave a shrug. "And it wasn't exactly a 'display.' I was seated in my cube with my back to the doorway. No one who wasn't standing directly behind me in my cube could have seen or heard what I was doing. Nevertheless, it was wrong and I admit that."

She sat back and looked down at her papers. "I've discussed this with some others here in H.R." Crap, she'd probably told everyone she knew about this.

Mitchell wanted to slide out of the chair and dig a hole to crawl into. He'd be the butt of jokes for weeks, if he still had a job. He wasn't sure what was worse—no job, or losing the respect he'd spent years building among his co-workers. Mitchell had worked hard to keep his personal life private and to avoid any suggestion of inappropriate behavior.

"And?" He braced himself for the worst.

"The company would like you to attend counseling. We feel, as does your supervisor, that you are a valuable employee, and that this was just a lapse of judgment. However, there must be steps taken to legally satisfy the corporation."

"Counseling?" He let out his breath. That was a new one. "Why would I need counseling?"

"Well, you'd only have to go a few times. Just to talk to the psychologist." She smiled at him. "About your problem."

"But, I don't have a problem." Well, he did, but it wasn't something he could talk about to a shrink. What could he say about Sammi and their incredible relationship? Would anyone ever believe it? He'd look crazier than just jerking off at work, that's for sure.

She shrugged. "It's that or dismissal."

Mitchell nodded. "All right. Counseling it is."

"And, you will be on probation for ninety days."

Mitchell slumped in his chair. "What does that mean exactly?"

She leaned forward, slapped his folder shut. "It means, one wrong step and your employment with us will be terminated."

"I understand." He nodded and stood. She remained seated, pulled out another folder, and flipped it open. He left her office, confused, but glad he hadn't been fired.

Shit. Probation. One small screw-up before dismissal.

Taking a deep breath, he pressed the call button for the elevator. He'd toe the line, show up on time, put in his forty hours, turn in flawless reports, and even restrain himself from jerking off at his desk if it meant keeping his job.

But, counseling? He'd always thought of himself as steady, even tempered, and perhaps the sanest of his friends. All he had to do was go, just show up. No one could make him talk if he didn't want to talk. And he didn't want to talk, not when he wasn't sure if he really wanted to dissect his relationship, his odd connection, with Sammi.

No matter what the shrink said, he wasn't giving up Sammi.

* * *

Mitchell could hear the music before he even put his key in the lock. He opened the front door of his apartment and classical music blasted him.

"Sammi!" Mitchell tossed his keys on the hall table.

No answer. Down the hall, the door to the bedroom was shut. Mitchell did a quick sweep of the living room, dining room, and kitchen, but no Sammi. Quirking an eyebrow,

Mitchell headed for the bedroom, dying to know what waited for him behind the door.

His anticipation grew as he turned the knob and pushed open the door. The bedroom was empty, but he could hear the shower running in the bathroom. An image of Sammi, soapy, hot, and wet, filled Mitchell's mind and his cock twitched. Even though he couldn't wait to get his hands on Sammi, Mitchell took his time undressing, relishing the wait, letting the arousal build to achingly sweet heights. By the time he slipped out of his briefs, his cock was a rod of steel standing against his belly.

He opened the drawer, found the lube and a condom, and headed for the bathroom.

Steam filled the room; the mirror had fogged and obscured any reflections. The sound of water hitting Sammi's body made the atmosphere seem charged. Through the glass blocks of the double shower a vague shape moved as if swaying to some internal rhythm, a ghostly image sent to drive Mitchell wild. Underneath the patter of the shower, Mitchell heard Sammi's purr of pleasure. Closing his eyes, Mitchell opened himself up to his lover. A jolt of pleasure shot through him as Sammi's emotions filled him. Sammi was touching himself.

Join me.

Mitchell didn't need to be asked twice. After the day he'd had, all he'd wanted as he sat at his desk, as he drove home, and as he hunted through the house, was Sammi. Just a touch of the man he'd fallen in love with would make everything better.

Stepping around the opening of the glass blocks, Mitchell's feet hit the warmed tiles of the shower floor and he caught his first glimpse of his soul mate.

Sammi's back was to Mitchell. Water streamed over him, running down his skin, hugging the curves in the small of his back, dripping off the round globes of his tight ass, and coursed down his legs. Muscles flexed and bunched as Sammi ran the soap over his skin, leaving foamy paths that were quickly washed away.

Mitchell wanted to bathe Sammi with his tongue. Every inch. Every sweet spot. He wanted to hear Sammi moan, and feel all the pleasure their mating could produce.

Stepping up, Mitchell placed his arms on either side of Sammi, trapping him. Sammi leaned back, pressing his back into Mitchell's chest. Wet, heated skin contacted Mitchell's flesh, trapping his cock between them.

Sammi writhed against him. Damn, it was sweet. The connection between them strengthened and soared. Sammi's arousal fed into Mitchell and he nearly lost his load when Sammi began a slow, sudsy shimmy down Mitchell's body, then just as slowly, Sammi rose. It was sweet torture, and Mitchell's head fell back as he soaked up the feelings that washed over him like the water from the shower.

Mitchell leaned forward, pressing Sammi against the wall of glass. Sammi's hands, fingers splayed, left soft smears on the blocks, erasing the fog of the hot water, allowing small glimpses of the bathroom beyond. Then, the spaces fogged again and were lost.

As he knelt, Mitchell's hands ran down the sides of Sammi's body, along his lean flanks, over his muscled thighs and then up again, to discover the pulsing erection he wore like a proud staff, straight and thick. Sammi cried out and a jolt of sexual arousal shot through Mitchell. Sammi's hand clutched the soap and he shared it with Mitchell. Stroking Sammi's cock, together they spread the warm, soapy lather over his smooth balls and along the length of his glorious spear.

"Turn around."

Sammi obeyed. Mitchell loved that about Sammi. He could ask and Sammi would obey him as if all Sammi lived for was to please Mitchell. And he did please Mitchell, more than anyone had ever pleased him.

Sammi reached up and angled the showerhead to wash water over his body, rinsing his cock clean. Mitchell held it by the base of the shaft; his tongue darted out, and in a long, leisurely swipe, licked the perfect heart-shaped head of Sammi's erection.

Groaning, Sammi's hand delved into Mitchell's wet hair, working through it as he guided Mitchell's head. Mitchell licked up and down the shaft, then moved to Sammi's smooth balls. Mitchell could taste the musk of Sammi's sex. He sucked one ball into his mouth and Sammi fell back against the wall of the shower, his knees bent to keep himself upright, as Mitchell switched from left to right, pleasuring him.

Unable to stand it any longer, Mitchell took Sammi into his mouth, plunging deep to cover as much cock as he could take in his throat. Mitchell sucked hard as he pulled back. Sammi gasped. His legs quivered as his muscles strained to keep him upright as Mitchell gave him head.

Working like a demon on Sammi's cock, Mitchell's tongue flicked along the underside and drove Sammi's pleasure through the roof. As Mitchell's hands kneaded Sammi's ass, his strong fingers probed the cleft between Sammi's firm cheeks, running in a hard, demanding touch up and down the valley.

Sammi's knees failed, and with a cry he did a slow slide to the floor. Mitchell's mouth kept its grip on Sammi's cock, following it down. Relentless, Mitchell, on his hands and knees, pushed Sammi toward orgasm.

Together, they gathered the ecstasy building in each of them and blended it into an incredible ball of power, only to pass it back and forth between them. Mitchell's balls tightened, his cock strained and throbbed as muscles sent jism moving through his shaft, and he felt Sammi's building orgasm as it traveled down the length of his cock.

They exploded together. Sammi's cum filled Mitchell's mouth as he hungrily swallowed. Hot, musky, and salty, it washed down his throat. Mitchell shot his load, spilling on the floor of the shower. They lay on the floor, chests heaving as the water rained on them, Mitchell's head on Sammi's chest and Sammi holding him.

Damn, this desire for Sammi was going to kill Mitchell.

* * *

"We're going out tonight. No arguments," Mitchell said as he dressed. Sammi sat on the bed, a towel draped over his shoulders. The last thing he wanted was to go out, but he'd put Mitchell off too long. And Mitchell looked as if he really needed a night out.

"All right." Sammi started getting dressed. "But, I don't have any money."

"You don't need any," Mitchell said. "Not with me, babe."

No one had ever been so generous to Sammi, not without expecting something in return. Sammi knew Mitchell expected nothing that Sammi didn't already want to give.

In less than ten minutes, they were out the door and climbing into Mitchell's black Jetta.

"Nice car." Sammi sank into the seat, slouching low so no one could see him.

"It's okay. I'd really love a two-seater convertible. Like a Beemer." Mitchell grinned as he pulled away. "How about some Mexican?"

"Sounds good." Sammi watched the neon lights of Montrose as they drove. The farther they drove the better he felt.

He imagined him and Mitchell driving, traveling far away from Houston, in the convertible Mitchell dreamed of, the wind in their hair and the sun on their bare shoulders. Maybe Mitchell would take him on a trip. Sammi had never taken a vacation like the ones he'd seen on television.

At last, they pulled into a restaurant parking lot. Sammi had no idea where he was, but he knew they'd left Montrose behind. No chance he'd be spotted here. Relief surged through him and he got out of the car with a smile on his face. Mitchell smiled back.

"Where are we?"

"Inside the loop. This neighborhood is called the Heights. This restaurant is a hole in the wall, but it's great and they make killer margaritas." Mitchell seemed so sure of himself, so confident. It really turned Sammi on, and his cock began to rise, but they were in the restaurant and he didn't want to embarrass Mitchell.

They were seated, given menus, and Sammi scanned his. Everything looked great. He followed Mitchell's lead, and both of them ordered frozen margaritas and beef enchiladas.

"What happened at work?" Sammi asked after the waiter had left. He was worried that Mitchell had gotten into even more trouble.

"Not much. I'm on probation."

"What's that mean?" Sammi popped a salsa-laden chip into his mouth.

"I have to keep my nose clean and see a shrink." The waiter arrived with their food and their conversation stopped as he placed the hot plates in front of them. They dug in.

"A shrink? Really? What about?" Sammi continued.

"Well, it seems I have a problem that I can't control." Mitchell looked so serious that Sammi's belly began to clinch.

Sammi leaned forward. "What is it?" He'd never seen any sign of drug use or alcohol on Mitchell.

Mitchell lowered his voice so nearby diners couldn't hear him. "I keep getting a hard-on every time I think of you."

Sammi felt his cheeks burn, but he loved the compliment. "Me, too. I can barely keep my hands off you right now." He let a wicked grin spread over his face and he tossed his head, throwing his bangs back.

The hungry look in Mitchell's eyes told him everything. Through the rest of the meal looks passed between them that promised each other their hunger would be satisfied.

Through the rest of the meal they continued to chat, sharing their day with each other until the check came. Sammi had done nothing, really. He'd cleaned up the apartment, fixed some lunch, and watched television. The whole day had been his with no one to answer to, no one watching his every move or following him around. In Mitchell's apartment, he'd felt freer than he had in years.

Although Donovan had never put physical chains on Sammi, he'd kept him prisoner for a long time. At first, Sammi had been happy to play the young lover to the older man who'd rescued him from the streets.

They'd met in a gay bar. Sammi had focused in on Donovan and the rest was history. Donovan had given Sammi free run of the penthouse and use of the Town Car. Money was no problem either, and for Sammi, who'd never had anything, that had been seductive and intoxicating.

Then, Donovan changed the rules and Sammi's freedom disappeared in a single day. He'd been locked in the penthouse, under the watchful eyes of an armed guard who stood at the door day and night.

Donovan started a portfolio of photographs of Sammi. He'd pose Sammi on what had once been their bed and snap shot after shot, each more graphic than the next. Sammi understood that he was being used. It wasn't the first time. Although uneducated, Sammi wasn't stupid. He had enough street smarts to realize what was going on the first time that Donovan had brought several older men to the penthouse.

It was supposed to be a party.

Instead, they'd taken turns fucking Sammi, and when they weren't fucking him they were watching someone else fuck him. Sammi never saw it, but he was sure money had changed hands. He'd been a whore before, on the dark streets near the park. At least he'd made some money then and could come and go as he pleased.

After the men left, Sammi had asked Donovan about his share of the money. That was the first time Donovan had put Sammi in the closet. Whether in conversation or not, Donovan had found out about Sammi's fear of small places, and used it to punish and control him.

The closet was so small. And there was no light. The bulb had been removed and the doorframe weather-stripped so that no light shown around the edges. Sammi could stand or sit, but not lie down.

The sides of the closet had been too close around him. Walls had brushed his arms as he sat with his knees against his chest and his head resting on them. He'd tried closing his eyes, pretending he was somewhere else, but that only lasted so long before the walls had closed in on him.

Tears of fear had flowed and his mouth had contorted in a wasted scream as his lungs struggled to get enough air; his chest had tightened, and his heart had pounded as if it would explode. Unable to keep control, he'd beaten his fists on the wooden door until they'd been bruised and aching, but Donovan never released him.

Not until Donovan was ready and Sammi had been beaten into a pliant, obedient creature.

Donovan's creature.

And the next customers would arrive.

Chapter Five

As they drove back to Mitchell's, Sammi rolled his window down. The warm night air blew through his hair, and he could see glimpses of stars. Mitchell's hand rested on his leg, and the weight of it felt so solid, warm, and comforting. An incredible man loved him. Just for being him. It was a beautiful night.

Then the Mercedes pulled alongside. Sammi glanced at it briefly and then over at Mitchell. "How soon before we get home?"

"Not long. Why?"

"Just wondering." Sammi shrugged and slouched in his seat.

An odd feeling came over him, as if someone had run a sharp fingernail down his spine. He glanced out the window, but the Mercedes had dropped back. They couldn't get home fast enough for Sammi.

He glanced in the side mirror.

The Mercedes was two cars behind them now.

"I can't wait to get you home where we can have some privacy." Mitchell's hand gave his thigh a gentle squeeze.

"I know." Sammi turned and smiled at him.

Mitchell's profile was strong and handsome. His hair tossed in the wind and the slight shadow of his beard made him look sexier than sin. Sammi wanted to feel that stubble on his skin as it rubbed across his chest or on the tender skin of his cock. Sammi reached over and caressed the crease in Mitchell's leg where it met his hip. The beginning of Mitchell's erection was a lump under his trousers.

"That feels good," Mitchell purred. Sammi continued to rub and Mitchell continued to harden.

Sammi glanced at the side mirror again.

The Mercedes was only one car behind.

The fingernail ran down his spine again. Donovan had a Town Car, not a Mercedes. Sammi relaxed and smiled at Mitchell.

"You feel good to me." Sammi rubbed harder.

"I'm going to have an accident it you keep that up."

"Oh, sorry." Sammi pulled his hand away.

"I didn't mean for you to stop, just not be so intense." Mitchell chuckled.

"Okay." Sammi's hand returned to its place.

Sammi recognized the street and knew Mitchell would be turning the corner. He focused on the mirror and the Mercedes that loomed in it. Mitchell signaled, slowed, and made the turn.

The Mercedes glided past the street without turning.

Sammi let out the breath he was holding. After pulling up outside the house, Mitchell parked, and they got out and went upstairs.

Once inside, Mitchell pulled Sammi into his arms. "Come here, babe."

Sammi slid into his embrace. A perfect fit. Lifting his face to Mitchell, he opened his lips and took the kiss. Mitchell tasted of heaven, pure and warm and like spring rain in his mouth.

Another finger ran down his spine. Sammi pulled away.

"What's wrong?"

"Nothing." Sammi went to the window and peeked out of the curtain.

The Mercedes had pulled up outside.

Swallowing down his terror, Sammi turned to Mitchell. "Does this place have a back door?"

"Yeah. Why?"

"Because we need to get out of here. Now." Sammi tried to keep his voice calm, but by the widening of Mitchell's eyes, he hadn't succeeded.

"What are you talking about?" Mitchell's arms flew to his hips.

"Remember that guy I told you about? The one who beat me?"

Mitchell nodded.

"Well, he's been looking for me and if he finds me…" Sammi lost his words. He wasn't ready to tell the truth, not yet.

"Don't worry. I won't let him hurt you."

Sammi shook his head. "Mitchell, he's really big and strong. And he carries a gun. We need to go. Now." Sammi grabbed Mitchell's hand and started for the kitchen.

Mitchell followed, pulled along by the sudden strength in Sammi's grip. "Easy, babe, easy." Sammi found the door and tried to open it but it wouldn't budge.

A loud pounding on the front door began.

"Now! Open the door, Mitchell!" Sammi tugged on the knob in a near panic. They had to get out of there or Moretti would find them. Sammi would be returned to Donovan and he refused to think about what Moretti would do to Mitchell.

Sammi's ramped-up fear flooded Mitchell, triggering a primal flight-or-fight response. He flung himself forward and flipped the top deadbolt. The door flew open and Sammi lunged down the stairs in the dark. Mitchell clambered down the stairs, shutting the door as his front door exploded open.

Shit, what the hell was going on?

At the bottom of the stairs, Sammi opened the door and as Mitchell hit the bottom steps, they tumbled outside. Mitchell shut the door and stood in the dark of the backyard staring at Sammi.

"What's over that fence?" Sammi pointed to the rear fence. "Any dogs?"

Dogs? Mitchell was so confused. "No." He shook his head.

"Come on," Sammi whispered, as he ran for the fence.

Mitchell bolted. They reached the wooden fence and Sammi leapt, caught the top of the laths, and vaulted over.

Mitchell did the same. His heart hammered as he cleared the boards. Landing on his feet, he crouched on the ground in the darkness. Sammi knelt beside him and put his finger to his lips. Mitchell nodded. In a running crouch, Sammi made his way to the back gate as Mitchell followed. They were through the gate and onto the sidewalk of the next street before Mitchell even had time to catch his breath.

"What now?" Mitchell asked, his eyes darting up and down the street.

"We need to get away from here. Is there any place around here we can go?" Sammi's soft voice still trembled. This guy must be a big son of a bitch to have Sammi so scared. Mitchell caught his breath and looked around.

Brian.

"Come on; I have a friend who lives about six blocks away." Mitchell started jogging down the tree-lined street with Sammi on his heels.

Mitchell set an easy pace and Sammi jogged alongside him. They stuck to the sidewalks, but Sammi kept looking over his shoulder.

"Get down!" Sammi rasped.

Mitchell veered off and crouched behind a minivan parked in a driveway. Sammi clung to his side as if seeking shelter. Mitchell wrapped his arm around Sammi's shoulders and hugged the trembling man to him.

What the hell was going on? As soon as they got to Brian's, Sammi was going to have to answer some questions.

Headlights flashed and a pickup truck passed them. They exhaled, stood, and continued their jog through the neighborhood. At last, Mitchell turned down a street and slowed to a walk. They strolled the last block and climbed the short steps to a bungalow with the porch light on and an SUV parked in the drive.

Mitchell glanced at his watch and then knocked. It was late, but Brian rarely went to bed before midnight.

The door opened and light poured out onto the porch. "Mitchell? What are you doing here?" Brian stood in the doorway, his broad shoulders taking up most of its width.

"Glad to see you too." Mitchell grinned at his best friend.

"Sorry. You usually call. Come in." Brian stepped aside and Mitchell entered, his hand clasping Sammi's in a tight grip.

"I know it's late, but I need some help." Mitchell grimaced.

Brian nodded at Sammi. "Introduce me."

"Sorry. Brian, this is Sammi. This is my best friend, Brian Russell."

Brian's eyes flicked to Mitchell and Sammi's entwined hands and smirked. "And Sammi is what to you?" He shut the door and followed them into the living room. Plopping down onto a brown leather couch, he motioned for them to sit.

"Sammi is my lover. He's living with me." Mitchell fell onto the loveseat opposite the couch and dragged Sammi down with him. Sammi slid under his arm and snuggled against Mitchell's side.

"When did this happen?" Brian raised his brows and cocked his head at Mitchell. Brian was the first person

Mitchell would have told about Sammi, but there hadn't been any time before tonight. He'd been so lost in Sammi for the last—oh God, had it only been two days?

"We met two nights ago. At a bar." Mitchell gave Brian a wry grin. "I know, I know, I swore off bars and everything, but…" He glanced at Sammi and shrugged.

"Wow. This is kind of sudden, isn't it?" Brian sat back and crossed his leg over his knee.

"Yeah, I know, but it just feels so right. I never thought I'd feel like this again." Mitchell flashed Sammi a smile.

"I'm glad, Mitchell. It's been too long." They exchanged a look that said too much. It had been five years since Steve had died, leaving a hole in Mitchell that had never healed.

"It's wild." Mitchell raked his hand through his hair. "Anyway, someone broke into my house tonight." He didn't want to go into the entire mess; it sounded so sordid, and there would be enough time in the morning to go into it all. "We need a place to spend the night. I have to go to work in the morning."

"Sure. Not a problem. You two can take the back bedroom." Brian stood. "Looks like you could use something to drink. Coffee or wine? Or do you need a shot of whiskey?"

Mitchell looked at Sammi. Sammi was still on edge, but calming down. "Make it two glasses of wine. The good stuff, too, nothing with a screw top."

"You insult me, Mitchell. I thought you knew me better than that." Brian laughed and went to an antique painted cupboard that had been converted into a bar. He pulled out a bottle from the small wine cooler that had been fitted inside.

Like an expert, he pulled the cork and poured two glasses. Then, he reached for the whiskey and poured a drink for himself.

Sammi reached for his and took a tentative sip. "It's good."

Mitchell sipped, letting the dark red liquid dance over his tongue. "Thanks."

"Now," Brian said as he settled back on the couch. "Tell me everything."

"Not much to tell." Mitchell shrugged.

Brian looked at Sammi. "Is that so?"

Sammi looked up from over the lip of the wine glass, a smile just touching his full lips. His bangs obscured one side of his face. "Do you want the details or just the gist?"

Brian laughed and Mitchell joined him. "Just the gist. Spare me the details."

"We met at a bar two nights ago." Sammi's eyes flicked to Mitchell. "We've been fucking ever since," he purred.

Mitchell groaned and rolled his eyes.

Brian barked out a laugh. "Well, it's good to know you're back in the game."

"He's not back in the game. He's off the market," Sammi said, holding up his hand clasped firmly in Mitchell's. "He's mine," he calmly declared.

Mitchell took a quick gulp of his wine. "You tell him, babe."

Sammi leaned back and lifted his face to Mitchell. Mitchell sank into the kiss. Delicious. He sighed.

"Get a room, you two!" Brian laughed and stood. "You know where it is, the bath's down the hall. Help yourself to whatever. I'm going to bed." He tossed down the rest of his whiskey, gave them a nod, and disappeared.

"I like him," Sammi said.

"Me, too."

"He's your best friend?" Sammi's brow furrowed.

"Yeah, but we never slept together. We're strictly friends. I'm not his type," Mitchell assured him.

"What is his type?" Sammi asked.

"Brian prefers big blonds with more muscles than brains."

"Oh." Sammi nodded. "Does he have someone?"

"Not right now. But, I sure hope he finds the right guy, like I did."

"A soul mate?"

"Yeah, babe. A soul mate." Mitchell took Sammi's mouth in a deep kiss and let Sammi's arousal wash over him. "Let's hit the sack. And by that I mean just sleep. I'll be worth nothing if I don't get eight hours."

"Right. Probation." Sammi stood and pulled Mitchell to his feet. "But, after work, you're mine."

"Absolutely. Wild horses couldn't keep me away from you."

Mitchell led them down the hall to the back bedroom. After showering separately, they slid under the covers and held each other. Sammi fit so perfectly tucked against his body. Mitchell felt the rise and fall of Sammi's chest, his soft breathing, the steady pounding of his heartbeat. Contentment filled Mitchell.

This was too good to be true.

When would the bubble burst and reality surge over them? More than anything, he wanted forever with Sammi, but even he had to admit their situation was odd.

What would the shrink have to say about it?

Chapter Six

In the morning, Mitchell sat with the guys at the breakfast table, sipping coffee. Sammi wore the same clothes he'd worn for the last week. Mitchell, unshaven, wore only briefs and a T-shirt he'd been lucky to find in a drawer. Brian, dressed in jeans with a white dress shirt over them, looked totally handsome, as always. Mitchell envied Brian's knack of knowing how to put himself together.

"I need to borrow some of your clothes, man." Mitchell gave Brian a shrug.

"No problem. Take what you need. Won't be the first time."

Mitchell smiled at him in thanks. "Now, I have a huge favor to ask."

"Ask away. Doesn't mean I'll do it." Brian took a sip from a mug that said "Cowboy Butts Drive Me Nuts".

Mitchell opened his wallet, pulled out two hundred dollar bills and handed them to Brian. "If your schedule is clear, would you take Sammi and buy him some clothes? Jeans, shirts, briefs, socks, the whole works."

"Where are your clothes?" Brian turned to Sammi.

"I don't have any. I left them when I left the jerk." Sammi took a sip.

"You must have really wanted out." Brian's eyes narrowed.

"You have no idea." Sammi grimaced.

"You need my car?" Brian asked Mitchell.

"No, I'm calling a cab. Back in a few." Mitchell stood and headed off to find some clothes. He planned to have the cab stop by his apartment to check it out. At least secure the busted door, that is, if there was anything left to secure. The thought of his place open all night long made him sick. No telling who had been in there.

He showered, shaved, and picked out clean slacks and a shirt, but reused his tie. His socks and briefs could stay. He'd grab some fresh ones at the house. Dressed, he rejoined the men in the kitchen.

"Okay, I'm ready."

"I called the cab for you," Brian said.

"Thanks, man. I mean it. I don't know what I'd have done without you." Mitchell shook his head.

"You'd have gone to a hotel."

"I didn't even think of that." Mitchell rolled his eyes.

"That break-in must have really shaken you up last night."

Mitchell glanced at Sammi, silently listening to their conversation.

"I guess it did."

"I'm hoping you'll tell me everything when you get home, Mitchell." Brian's eyes told him that he'd have to explain a lot more than he'd shared last night.

"Promise." Brian deserved the truth for taking them in.

Sammi stood and followed Mitchell to the door. "I'll miss you. But, I promise I won't call." Sammi smiled up at him.

Mitchell cupped Sammi's chin and raised it. His lips pressed against Sammi's and he sighed into them. "Miss you."

He opened the door and left.

Sammi turned around and went back to the kitchen. He slipped into the chair as Brian refilled his cup.

"Well, where do you want to go shopping?" Brian watched him as if he were looking for some answers. Sammi wasn't sure if he trusted Brian, even though Mitchell did. Trust came hard for Sammi.

"I don't." Sammi shook his head. "I don't want Mitchell to spend his money on me."

"Do you have any money?" Brian sat back and wrapped his arm over the back of his chair.

"No." Sammi frowned. There was only one way he'd ever known how to earn money and he'd never sell himself again, not now that he had Mitchell.

"Then, for now, let Mitchell take care of you. It seems you need it."

"I'll pay him back. Every dime." He would even though he had no idea how.

"I don't think he cares if you do. Mitchell is a very generous, loving person."

"Your best friend." Sammi looked at Brian and smiled.

"That's right. I don't want to see him hurt, Sammi. He's had enough of that." Brian stared into this mug.

Sammi brushed his bangs back. "How?" Sammi had felt the sadness in Mitchell the first time he'd heard Mitchell's thoughts. His loneliness and pain had been so close to the surface, so very raw.

"Did he tell you about Steve?"

"No." Sammi leaned forward.

"Seven years ago, Mitchell met Steve. They were together for two and a half years. Then Steve died."

Sammi's heart ached for Mitchell. "AIDS?"

"No, killed by a drunk driver. Steve had stopped to change a flat tire on the Interstate. The car ran into the back of his car and he was caught between them." Brian's voice had lowered to a near whisper. Sammi felt Brian's pain, still so fresh and aching, that it shocked him. That kind of pain meant deep feelings.

Sammi frowned. "Did you know Steve?"

"Yes." Brian looked at his feet.

"Did you love him?" Sammi whispered.

Brian looked up into Sammi's face. "Yes. Don't tell Mitchell. He doesn't know and I never said anything. Steve belonged with Mitchell. Please. I shouldn't have told you." He shook his head. "I don't know how you figured that out."

"It's a gift." Sammi reached out and touched Brian's hand. "I won't tell Mitchell. Promise." That sort of thing was best left unsaid; even Sammi knew that much.

"Thanks." Brian stood. "Let's go shopping."

"Can't you just pick some things out for me? I'm terrible at that stuff and I really don't like going out. Large crowds bother me," Sammi pleaded.

For a minute it looked like Brian would refuse, then he sighed. "Okay. Write down your sizes." Brian gave Sammi a slip of paper and a pen. "Jeans okay?"

"That's fine." Sammi scribbled his information and handed the paper to Brian. "Thanks."

"I understand about the phobia stuff. For me, it's snakes. I hate snakes." Brian shuddered. "Make yourself at home. I'll be back in a couple of hours."

Sammi stood. "You're a really good friend, Brian. Thanks for taking us in."

"I took Mitchell in. You were with him." Brian leaned forward, his hands on the back of the chair. "He loves you. I can see the attraction. You're just his type."

"What type is that?" Sammi asked from under his dark bangs.

"Sexy as hell and nothing but trouble," Brain drawled, shook his head, and left.

Sammi leaned back. Brian had nailed it. That was Sammi's life story.

Sex and trouble.

* * *

Mitchell stepped out of the cab and stared at the two flat tires on his car. Shit. Someone hadn't wanted them to use it to get away. His eyes tracked up the stairs to his front door. It was shut, or appeared to be shut.

"Wait for me," he told the driver. "I'll only be a few minutes."

He trotted up the stairs to the door. The frame had split, but the door had been pulled closed. Thank God for small favors. He pushed it open and waited. Silence.

Stepping inside, he saw what was left of the ceramic bowl he kept his keys and loose change in. Shards of it were strewn across the floor. Stepping over the pieces, he moved farther inside and surveyed the damage.

Exhaling deeply, Mitchell's shoulders fell. Not as bad as he'd thought, but bad enough. Nothing was gone, but everything that could be thrown and smashed, was. Debris littered the living room floor.

Someone had been really pissed off.

He moved into the kitchen. The back door stood open. He'd closed it, so whoever had done this had figured out where he and Sammi had fled. In the hall, he checked out his study. The computer looked untouched, thank God.

The taxi was waiting so Mitchell hurried to his bedroom. The bed had been tossed, and his clothes lay strewn on the floor. Going to his chest, he pulled out a handful of briefs and socks, then grabbed a pair of jeans from the floor and a few shirts.

When he entered the bathroom, he froze.

"I want him back" was scrawled on his mirror with black marker. Beneath it was "Donovan". Its starkness and the implied threat sent fear knifing through him.

Donovan wanted Sammi back. What an odd way to say "I love you, come home." It sounded as if Sammi had been stolen property that Mitchell should return instead of a runaway lover.

Gathering the last of his things and a duffle bag to stuff them into, Mitchell headed out of the house and climbed into the cab. He'd come back this afternoon and call the cops to report the break-in, then call his insurance agent. Right now, he needed to get to work on time.

* * *

Sammi pulled a denim shirt from the back of Brian's chair and slipped it on. He'd found a blue bandana in the dresser and with a quick swipe, he pushed back his bangs and tied the cloth around his head, pulling it low over his forehead.

On his way out the door, he snagged Brian's sunglasses and put them on. Disguise complete. After locking the door behind him, Sammi trotted down the steps and headed toward Montrose Avenue.

Thirty minutes later, he stood outside the building. Taking a deep breath, he entered. The waiting room was small and bare, with a dozen metal folding chairs around the walls. Several men and two women waiting their turns glanced up at him. The men checked him out; the women went back to their magazines. Ignoring the appreciative stares of the guys, Sammi walked to the counter and pressed a button near a frosted window.

It slid open and a woman shoved a clipboard at him.

"First name only, please."

Sammi wrote his name and pushed it back at her. She took it and looked at his name. "Take a seat, please. Your name will be called soon."

Sammi doubted that. The others in the room had the look of people who'd been there for some time. He had hoped he'd return before Brian did, but if not, he'd just say he'd gone for a walk.

The room emptied and filled with a new collection of people.

The door opened and a woman dressed in blue scrubs glanced at a clipboard.

"Sammi."

He stood and followed her inside. She walked to a scale.

"Height and weight."

He stepped onto the scale. "One hundred sixty-seven pounds." She raised a metal staff above his head, flipped out a shorter bar, and read off the measurement. "Five feet ten inches." She scribbled the information on the papers trapped under the clamp of the clipboard. "This way please." She led him to a small room.

Sammi paused at the doorway and looked in. Small, but not too small. Another deep breath and he stepped in.

"Up on the table." Sammi hopped up and looked around the room. Ahead of him was a blank green wall. A small counter with a sink and some medical supplies lined one side of the room near the door. Other than a stool, the rest of the room was empty.

"Take off the shirt, please. I need your blood pressure." Sammi slipped it off. She pushed the sleeve of the T-shirt up, took his arm and wrapped a long wide strip of plastic around it, and began pumping. The cuff puffed up and tightened on his arm.

"It hurts," he said.

"It's supposed to." She stopped pumping and he watched the needle on the dial go down as the cuff relaxed. "Temperature." She held up a thermometer on a curly cord. Sammi opened his mouth and she placed it under his tongue. After a few seconds, it beeped and she pulled it out.

"I need some medical history."

"Okay." Sammi licked his lips, sucked the bottom one into his mouth, and chewed on it.

"How old are you?"

"Twenty-three."

"When was the last time you saw a doctor?"

"A long time ago."

"How old were you?"

"Ten, I guess."

"Did you get shots then?"

"I think so."

"Why do you want to see the doctor?"

"I want to get a checkup. And a blood test."

"We'll do that after the doctor sees you."

"Okay."

She finished writing and went to the door. "Someone will be in to see you in a few minutes." She left.

Sammi stared at the wall. It was the ugliest shade of green he'd ever seen. All the walls were cracked. His gaze climbed upward. The ceiling was made of those big white tiles and the light was a cheap florescent fixture. The shadows of the bugs that had died in it formed patterns on the yellowed plastic.

The door opened and a young woman came in. "Hello. I'm Beth. The social worker." She sat on the stool and put her clipboard on the desk. "This is a free clinic and is funded by a variety of grants. One of those grants requires us to gather information about the patients for research. All the answers you give are anonymous. Please give the most honest answers possible. Okay?" Facing away from him, she bent over the desk to write.

"Okay." Sammi steadied his voice by focusing on a spot on the ugly green wall.

"Do you consider yourself heterosexual, homosexual, or bi-sexual?"

"Homosexual."

"Have you ever had sexual relations with someone of the opposite sex?"

"No."

"How old were you when you experienced your first sexual encounter? That can mean anything from a kiss to full intercourse."

"Ten."

"How old were you when you first had full intercourse?"

"Ten."

"Were you sexually abused as a child?"

"Yes."

"Was this by a family member, a trusted friend, or a stranger?"

"Family member."

"Was this ever reported to the authorities?"

"No."

"Did you ever tell your parents?"

"No. I was in foster care."

"Are you currently sexually active?"

"Yes."

"Are you in a monogamous relationship?"

"Yes."

"For how long?"

"Two days."

"How long was your longest monogamous relationship?"

"Three months."

"How many times in the last year have you had sexual relations? Zero to ten. Ten to twenty. Twenty to fifty. Fifty to one hundred. Over one hundred."

"Twenty to fifty."

"How many sexual partners have you had this year? Zero to ten. Ten to twenty. Twenty to fifty. Fifty to one hundred. Over one hundred."

"Twenty to fifty."

"Have you ever exchanged sex for money?"

"Yes."

"Is this your primary source of income?"

"Yes."

"What was your last year of school?"

"Eighth grade."

"Do you have a job?"

"No."

"Have you used a condom every time you've had sexual relations?"

"No."

"Just a few more questions. Have you ever taken drugs? That includes drugs like marijuana, cocaine, meth, and heroin."

"Yes."

"Did you take any drugs intravenously?"

"No."

"What drugs did you take?"

"Marijuana and cocaine."

"When was the last time you took either of those drugs?"

"Two years ago."

She checked off the last box and stood. "That's it. Thank you for participating. The doctor will be in to see you shortly."

"Okay." He'd just told a complete stranger more about his life than anyone else in the world knew, all condensed into a game of Twenty Questions.

After she left, Sammi chewed his lip and stared at the wall. It had a long crack that looked like a road going over another crack that looked like a hill. He and Mitchell might drive that road, go over hills, and maybe see some lakes or the beach. He'd never seen the beach. Or hills, for that matter.

The door opened and a man in a white coat stepped in. He wore blue plastic gloves. A nurse, also wearing gloves, followed, carrying a tray.

"Sammi? I'm Dr. Fowler."

"Hello, Dr. Fowler." Sammi sat up straight.

"I see from your forms that you haven't had any shots since childhood?"

"That's right."

"Okay. Well, there are several that I'll give you today."

"What for?" Sammi didn't like shots; that much he remembered.

"Hepatitis. Tetanus. Tuberculosis. Meningitis."

"I can't pay for them."

"All our services are free, Sammi." He smiled

"Okay." Sammi shrugged.

The nurse prepared a needle and handed it to the doctor. He gave Sammi the shot in his right arm. It hurt, but no worse than a bee sting. The nurse gave one to his left arm. Then they did it again. Both arms ached.

The doctor listened to Sammi's chest, his heart, had him breathe deeply several times, and felt his throat. Then Sammi lay back on the table and the doctor felt all over his belly.

"Stand up, face the table, and lower your pants and underwear. I need to do a rectal exam."

Sammi did what he was told.

"Just lean over."

He did. The doctor's fingers spread the cheeks of his ass apart and he slipped a cold, lubed plastic-clad finger inside Sammi. Sammi flinched as the doctor felt around, then pulled his finger out. Snapping off his glove and tossing it in the wastebasket, he slipped on a new one. Then, he cupped Sammi's balls and asked him to cough. He did.

Sammi had never had a man touch him down there without it being sexual. The doctor's touch was different and as matter-of-fact as the way he'd listened to Sammi's heart and lungs. It was very odd, but in a way, it made Sammi feel safe.

"Everything seems fine. You appear to be a completely healthy young man." The same patient smile. "Of course, the blood test will tell us everything. Nurse Wells will take some blood. Do you need any condoms today?"

"No."

"Well, then. Test results will be sent to an address you provide or you can pick them up. If there is any reason for you to return, we'll let you know. If not, I'll see you back here in a year." Another smile and he left.

The nurse pulled Sammi's arm out straight.

"Now, let's get some blood." She pulled a rubber tube out of her pocket and tied it around his arm. "Make a fist and pump."

He did. She searched for a vein and Sammi braced himself.

He'd never thought going to the doctor would hurt so much and he wasn't even sick. At least, he didn't think he was sick.

The blood test would tell everything.

Chapter Seven

The phone rang and Mitchell answered. "Mitchell Collins."

"Mr. Collins. Someone is here for you." The receptionist's voice wavered.

"Who is it?"

"He said to tell you Donovan sent him," she whispered, sounding more than a little scared.

"I'll be down shortly." Mitchell hung up and rolled his chair back. How the hell had this guy found him? Of course. The guy had been in his house, searching through all of his things. The fact that he knew who Mitchell was and had come to his office didn't bode well.

Shit. He did not need this crap and certainly not at the office.

Mitchell headed to the elevator. All the way down, dread filled him.

The door opened and Mitchell stepped into the large reception area. A round desk stood in the middle of the room, couches and tables arranged around it. At the window, with his back to Mitchell, stood a huge man. Light reflected off his shaved head, and his massive shoulders and arms looked as if he could crush more than just beer cans. No wonder Sammi didn't want this guy to catch up to him, or for Mitchell to go toe-to-toe with him, either.

"I'm Mitchell Collins." He didn't extend his hand, but stood with his arms at his sides. Sammi had said the man carried a gun. For a second, Mitchell wondered if he'd be shot down right here in the waiting room.

The man turned, and cold, steel grey eyes fell on Mitchell. There was nothing behind them—no emotion, no signs of humor, just coldness.

Ruthlessness.

A killer's eyes.

No wonder the receptionist was scared. The guy scared the shit out of Mitchell.

"You have something that belongs to Donovan," a deep bass voice rumbled. "He would like it returned."

The receptionist was staring at both men, her head moving from one to the other, her eyes wide. Mitchell prayed she was calling security.

"I don't think it wants to go back." Mitchell wanted to keep this entire mess on the down low, but it seemed it was going to play out here. "Tell Donovan to forget about it."

"Donovan wants his property returned or else." The man took a slow walk around the perimeter of the room. He reached the desk and with a careless flick of his hand, he swept a large vase filled with flowers onto the floor. It shattered and the receptionist jumped and muffled a scream. Hitting the keypad on the phone, she began dialing.

Mitchell hoped security or the cops would get here soon. Like before this big bastard killed him. No matter what, Mitchell wasn't turning Sammi over to anyone.

"Tell him to call the police and report it stolen." Where the hell all this bravery was coming from, Mitchell had no idea, but the words had just come out, as if someone else had control of his mouth.

Another flick of the hand and a lamp exploded on the tiles. The poor girl leapt from her chair and ran toward the elevators. Where the hell was security?

Mitchell stood his ground as the big man advanced.

"Donovan prefers to take care of these matters in private."

"This isn't exactly private." Mitchell motioned around the room.

"This is a request."

"What was last night?" He stared into the man's eyes.

"A repossession." Not a glimmer of a smile or any other emotion showed on his face. He was like a fucking robot. "Next time, it'll be a take down."

"There won't be a next time."

"Donovan knows where you live, where you work, and what you are."

At the unveiled threat, Mitchell's eyes narrowed and then darted to the half dozen other people, including Ms. Jane Walker from H.R., who had gathered at the commotion.

Shit. Double shit and crap.

She gawked at the big man, then her stare slid to Mitchell and her eyes narrowed.

"Tell Donovan to stay away from me. He can't have it back."

"Over your dead body?" One side of the goon's lips curled up in a wolfish grin.

Mitchell swallowed. "Something like that."

Security arrived, thank God. The big man looked at the gathering crowd. The guards didn't seem to know what to do with him.

"It would be my pleasure to insure that happens, you fag," he sneered.

All heads swiveled to Mitchell. Dozens of eyes widened. Fuck, he'd just been "outed" at work in front of a half dozen co-workers.

Could this get any worse?

Donovan's henchman sauntered through the crowd. Everyone stepped away from him, even the guards. Then, all eyes fell on Mitchell and the destroyed waiting area. How was he going to explain this?

"Mr. Collins, come with me." Ms. Walker found her voice and motioned him to the elevator as the receptionist returned and began picking up the mess.

Mitchell sighed and followed. This definitely counted as "one wrong step."

The ride up to her office was tense and silent. What she had to say to him would be done in the privacy of her office, but he knew what was coming. By now, the events that had just occurred downstairs would be making its journey along the office grapevine.

He trailed behind her as the people they passed sat up and took notice. In her office, Mitchell didn't wait to be asked to sit. He slumped into the chair.

"Can you explain what just happened?" Ms. Walker rubbed the bridge of her nose as if dealing with Mitchell gave her a headache.

She should feel the pounding in his head.

"That was unfortunate," he began. "I've never seen or met that man before today. He's someone who works for my lover's ex. Seems I'm caught up in a complicated love triangle."

"Right. You people are certainly flamboyant, if nothing else. All high drama." She pursed her lips at him.

"If you mean homosexuals, that is a generalization," Mitchell pointed out. Okay, some of the gay men he knew could be guilty of that, but he certainly wasn't, and neither were most of his friends who were gay, like Brian.

"I'm sorry to say it, Mr. Collins, but your employment here is terminated. That type of display will not be tolerated. Bringing your sordid sex life to work will not be condoned."

Mitchell stood. He'd had enough and he didn't intend to listen to some speech about inappropriate behavior. This was bullshit.

"Ms. Walker, in the last twenty-four hours my apartment has been vandalized, I've been chased from my home, my life threatened, and I've been 'outed' at work. Now you're firing me. My life is going down the crapper in a flush of cosmic proportions. I'm sure somewhere inside you there is a scrap of humanity, so I'm going to ask you to reconsider. I value my career and had no intention of stepping out of line." Mitchell swallowed. "I wish you would think about this again."

She raked her eyes over him and he could see the dislike in them. He just bet she thought "all the good ones are taken or gay."

"I'm sorry. My decision is final. You have thirty minutes to clean out your desk and leave the building."

Mitchell left her office. Eyes tracked him down the hall to the elevators.

It was a long ride to his floor and the elevator seemed to stop on every floor as he endured the stares of everyone who got on or off.

Mitchell wove his way to his cube.

On his desk sat a box of tissues and a small bottle of baby oil.

Ignoring his co-workers high school antics, he gathered his few personal possessions and shoved them into a plastic bag he pulled from his bottom drawer, picked up his duffle bag, and left. At the elevator, a small group of co-workers waited for him. His boss was not among them, nor was he anywhere to be found.

"It's just wrong, Mitchell. We can't believe they're doing this to you."

"You should fight it. Take them to court. It's discrimination."

"Hang in there. If there is anything you need, let me know."

All the kind words and worried smiles disappeared as the doors to the elevator shut and whisked Mitchell on a non-stop ride to the bottom.

* * *

The SUV was in the drive. Sammi trudged up the stairs and knocked on the door. He felt a slight twinge from the muscles where he'd gotten his shots.

Brian answered. "Sammi. Where the hell have you been?"

"Sorry, I should have left a note. I went for a walk." He shrugged as he entered. "I had a lot of stuff to think over."

Brian nodded. "Want to see what I got you?"

Sammi smiled. "Yeah. I'm sure it'll be great. You have such good taste."

"How do you know that?" Brian laughed as he got the bags.

"Well, you're Mitchell's best friend. And you look incredible." Sammi folded his legs under him as he sat on the couch and began to dig through the bags.

From the first large bag, Sammi pulled out jeans, T-shirts, and a couple of denim shirts. Socks and two packs of briefs were in another bag, along with aftershave, a nice razor—not one of those plastic kinds—and a deodorant stick that matched the aftershave. He spun the top on the aftershave and sniffed. It smelled like citrus with an underlying musk scent. Sammi couldn't wait to wear it for Mitchell.

"This is great. It'll be great to get out of these clothes." He scooped it all up and dashed down the hall before Brian could think of anything else to ask.

In the shower, Sammi began to feel odd. Just a few minutes before, he'd been happy. Now, sadness washed over him. He washed his hair and rinsed off. As he shaved, the feeling of melancholy grew more intense.

Shit. Something had happened to Mitchell, and with gut-wrenching certainty, Sammi knew it probably had to do with him. How much more could he screw up Mitchell's life?

He dressed in fresh clothes and headed back to the kitchen. Brian stood at the stove, preparing lunch. It smelled wonderful and despite his emotions, Sammi's stomach rumbled.

"What's that? It smells delicious."

"Glad you approve. It's lunch. Spaghetti and meat sauce."

"I love spaghetti." He pulled out a chair and dropped into it. "How did you learn to cook?"

"I've been on my own for a long time." Still facing the stove, Brian kept talking. "You just pick it up. It's not like I went to school for it."

"But you went to school." He tried to keep the envy from his voice. "College, right?"

"Yeah. Up in Austin at the University of Texas. That's where I met Mitchell. We had some classes together. Started hanging out."

"But you never hooked up?"

"No. Sex fucks up friendships."

Sammi didn't have much experience with friendship.

"What do you do?" Sammi was curious about the man who figured so prominently in Mitchell's life.

"Well, my degree is in engineering. But, now, I'm a P.I."

"A private detective? That's cool. How'd you learn that?"

"Took some law enforcement classes." The big man shrugged his shoulders. "Thought for a while I'd be a cop. But, the gay thing just wasn't happening. So, I turned it into a detective agency."

"You and Mitchell are so smart." Sammi bit his lip. Not like him. No education, just his street smarts, and most of those he wanted to forget.

"You seem like a pretty smart guy, Sammi. Don't underestimate yourself." Brian plated the spaghetti, and poured the meat sauce into a large bowl. "Hey, over in that cabinet, get us a couple of plates. The silverware is in that drawer."

Sammi set the table, careful to place the napkins in the correct positions. At the penthouse, all the meals were formal. Donovan insisted. Even though the kitchen had a counter and stools to sit on, Sammi had never been allowed to eat at it, not even a sandwich.

Brian pulled out the wine from last night and poured them each a glass.

They sat, passed the food around, and then dug in.

After his first few bites, Sammi said, "Something's wrong with Mitchell."

Brian looked up from his plate. "What are you talking about?"

"I can feel it. He's upset about something."

Brian put down his fork and picked up his glass. Sipping the wine, he looked at Sammi over the rim. "That gift of yours?"

Sammi squirmed in his seat. "Yeah."

Brian put down the glass and folded his arms. "You know, in my line of work you see a lot of common things. Life. Death. Love. Hate. Greed." His eyes bored into Sammi's. "Sometimes, you see things you can't explain."

Sammi took another drink of wine. He wanted Brian to stop staring at him as if he could see inside him. Sammi's eyes flicked to Brian's face.

"Do you have a gift?" Sammi asked.

A slow smile turned the corners of Brian's mouth up, making a killer set of dimples. "Some might call it that. I get feelings when I'm working. Whether someone is telling the truth or lying, whether I'm on the right trail, even what might have happened. Some people call it a hunch or a gut feeling. But it's much stronger than that. It's as if I can see it happening."

For a moment, Sammi thought Brian was bullshitting him, but the man was so serious, so sincere. He opened his emotions and picked up traces of Brian. Curiosity. Confidence. Sincerity.

"I can feel other people's emotions. Sometimes," Sammi said in a rush.

Brian nodded. "Thought so. Do you use it often?"

"Sometimes." He ducked his head and took a bite of spaghetti as Brian watched.

"Sometimes, huh?" Brian didn't look as if he believed Sammi at all.

"The food is delicious. I wish I could cook." Sammi smiled around a mouthful of food. "So I could cook for Mitchell. I want to make myself useful. I don't want him to think I'm taking advantage of him. I want to earn my keep."

"That's a good idea. Well, I could show you a few things. I happen to know some of Mitchell's favorite dishes." Brian's eyes twinkled.

"That would be great."

Sammi and Brian fell silent. Sammi was learning so much, about himself and about Mitchell. Even Brian. Sammi had never known so many people he felt comfortable around and trusted.

He could get used to this life.

If Donovan would ever let him go.

Chapter Eight

Mitchell got out of the cab, the plastic bag clutched in his fist and the duffle bag slung over his shoulder. He trudged up the stairs to his apartment. Pushing open the door, he headed straight to the kitchen. He dropped his bags, pulled open a drawer, and found his address book.

Flipping through the pages, he located the number of his insurance agent.

The room spun. He leaned on the counter and closed his eyes. Waves of nausea raced over him, his stomach clenched, and he rushed to the sink and vomited. Shaking as he leaned over the sink, he turned the tap, rinsing the meager contents of his stomach down the drain. He cupped his hands, sipped some water, and rinsed his mouth. Tremors started in his legs and arms, then spread to his entire body.

Unable to raise his head, Mitchell clung to the side of the sink and tried to get the shaking under control. Water running from the tap and the pounding in his head drowned out the eerie silence of what had once been a sanctuary for him.

The shivers stopped. He splashed cold water on his perspiration-drenched face. After turning off the tap, he pulled out a chair from the table and sat before his legs gave out.

Shit. Shit. Shit. Shit.

Mitchell leaned forward, elbows on the table, and cradled his head in his hands. It pounded like a son of a bitch. His life, once so calm and predictable, had become a fucking roller coaster ride since he'd met Sammi. Long slow climbs to the summits of ecstasy, then breakneck speed plunges to the bottom, then up again to career around hairpin turns, and then shoot through a blackened tunnel. Making love with Sammi had been more wonderful than he'd ever experienced, even his times with Steve. But, at what price?

Would he ever come out of the tunnel and into the light?

If he didn't give up Sammi, Donovan's goon would probably kill him. They had him by the balls. They knew his name, his address, his phone number. If they'd been in his computer, they probably knew his bank account.

Oh, shit.

Mitchell pushed to his feet and staggered to the study. As he sat in the chair, he turned on his PC and sat back to wait as it fired up. More than before, it felt as if it took forever to boot up. His fingers tapped the mouse pad as he waited. At last, the familiar jingle sounded and he put his hand on the mouse.

His desktop came up and icons popped into place. My Bank sat there, plain as day. Swallowing, he double-clicked it. His sign-in and password appeared already in place. He'd used the option to remember them. He hit log-in. The bank connected.

Clicking on Balance, he stared unbelieving at the screen.

Twenty-five dollars remained.

Fuck. He'd just deposited his paycheck. Even the extra cash cushion he kept for emergencies was gone. He clicked on Transaction History. His money had been transferred to another other account. They'd wiped him out.

A growing fear gnawed at his belly. He closed the window and clicked on the icon for one of his two credit cards.

He'd used the save I.D. and password there, too. How could he be so fucking stupid?

Mitchell clicked one open and hit the log-in.

Access Denied and Account Not Available flashed in red. They'd closed his account and fucked him royally. He didn't bother looking at the other credit card.

"Shit!" He stood and in a fury that swelled in him and then exploded, he wiped his desk clean, sending papers, a pencil holder, all its contents, and several books crashing to the floor.

"Damn that bastard!"

Mitchell's eyes filled with tears, but he fought them back. Sucking in a ragged breath, he straightened and let it out in a long, slow exhalation that emptied his lungs. Another deep breath and slow release.

He pulled his cell phone from his pocket, hit 9-1-1, and waited.

"I'd like to report a burglary."

* * *

Donovan watched as Moretti crossed the plush carpet with silent footsteps and placed a Fed-Ex envelope on his desk. Picking it up, Donovan looked at the front of it. The sender's address was a street in Rome. He smiled and ignored it. His intermediary would be too careful to put the real address on any paperwork that could be traced.

Opening it, he let the contents fall out. A slip of paper and an Italian passport hit the desk. He picked up the passport and flipped to the front of it. Sammi's face looked back at him. The paperwork looked perfect.

Sammi Constanza. As good a name as any for a man with no past.

As long as Sammi didn't officially exist, Donovan held the power. Sammi's last name had been lost in a sea of foster parents. With no birth certificate, that meant no name, and that meant no social security number, and a social security number meant everything.

Donovan tossed the passport down and picked up the paper. It was a deposit slip for two hundred and fifty thousand dollars for his offshore account.

Part one of the transaction was complete.

He double-clicked the mouse and brought up his email. Clicking on New, he typed, "Papers received. Item will be shipped in three days", added the address, then clicked Send, and sat back.

Donovan's eyes flicked to Moretti, standing at ease against the wall near the door.

"We have three days to find him and get him on that plane."

"Yes, sir." Moretti's eyes didn't move.

"Mitchell Collins?"

"Taken care of. I shut him down. No money, no credit, and by now, no job."

Donovan smiled.

Mitchell Collins would understand what it meant to take what belonged to Donovan and what it cost.

* * *

The police cruiser pulled up. Mitchell, sitting on the steps, didn't bother to stand as the cop got out.

"You called about the break-in?" the officer called to him.

"Yeah." Mitchell nodded. "I think they slashed my tires, too."

The officer stopped, circled Mitchell's car, took out a small camera, and shot a photo. He came up the steps, camera and clipboard in his hands. "I need some info first."

"Sure." As the cop leaned against the railing, Mitchell gave him all the details, omitting that fact that he and Sammi had been there when it happened last night, not today.

The cop left him on the stairs and checked out the door. "A kick-in."

Smart cop. Mitchell kept his tendency to be a smart ass in check and his mouth shut. "That's what I thought."

"Did you go inside?"

"Yeah. I checked it out, then called you."

"Did you touch anything?"

"Yeah. I checked my computer. They got to my bank account."

"Bad break." The cop grimaced and went inside.

Thirty minutes later, Mitchell sat on the stairs holding the police report. He'd need it for the insurance.

Exhausted and wrung out, he got to his feet and went back inside. Sitting in the kitchen, he dialed the insurance agent and gave him all the information. Since the guy handled his renter's and car insurance, he mentioned the car's flat tires. The agent told him to get them fixed and send him the bill.

Mitchell hung up. How was he going to pay for anything with no money and no credit cards? He'd given the last of his cash to Brian to buy clothes for Sammi. He'd have to wait for his final paycheck to clear at the end of the month before he had any money. There were savings, but it was through the company and with all the red tape, it would be over a week before he could have some money sent to him.

He gathered up the duffle bag and headed to Brian's house.

* * *

Sammi sat on the couch watching television and chewing his thumb. Mitchell would be here soon and Sammi dreaded finding out what had happened. Brian had disappeared into his office after lunch, leaving Sammi to occupy his time in whatever way he'd wanted.

At the penthouse, he hadn't had much free time. Donovan insisted he work out every day. There was a workout room, complete with weights, treadmill, and one of those contraptions that worked your entire body. Moretti would put him through his routine like a drill sergeant until the sweat poured off Sammi's body.

Then, he'd shower, change, and go to his room. It was large, but bare. No television, no computer, no video games. Donovan controlled all of that. Sammi was rewarded when Donovan felt he'd done well, like pleasing a client. As if he were some dog doing a trick, Donovan would hold out a treat for Sammi to jump at, usually a video to watch.

And like a good pet, Sammi jumped.

The alternative was the closet. And Sammi would do whatever it took not to be put in the closet.

He stretched out on the couch, his hand trailing over his belly, thinking of Mitchell. Mitchell had offered him everything, no strings attached, no treats to beg for, no punishments if he said no. Even Brian hadn't demanded anything of him, but left him to his own, treating him like an adult, not a child or a pet that had to be managed.

Freedom was so much better. He didn't care what he had to do; he was never going back to Donovan. If things got much worse, Sammi had no idea how long Mitchell would let him stay. Soul mate or not, Sammi feared Mitchell would leave him. Everyone who had ever mattered had walked away from him without a glance back over their shoulders.

If there was one thing Sammi knew, it was that he didn't deserve a man like Mitchell and, at some point, the rug would be pulled out from under his feet and Sammi would be left alone again.

He sat up. Maybe he should leave before that happened. More importantly, he should leave before Donovan caught up with him and made Mitchell pay for hiding him.

Getting lost should be easy in a big city like Houston.

Sammi went to his room and gathered what Brian had bought him. He stripped a pillowcase from the bed and stuffed everything inside. Then he tied on the bandana.

Pausing, he looked around the room. Should he leave a note? Fuck, what would he say to Mitchell?

It's been fun?

Thanks for everything?

It's better this way?

Forgive me?

No note could hold what was in his heart.

Sammi tossed the pillowcase over his shoulder and went to the door. Peeking out, he listened, then slipped to the front door. Brian was still in his study and it would be hours before Mitchell came home.

Sammi pulled the door softly closed and trotted down the steps. Striding as if he had a purpose, he made his way toward Montrose, every step taking him farther and farther from the man he loved and needed more than anything he'd ever known.

* * *

Mitchell knocked on Brian's front door. All he wanted was to sit down, put his feet up, and have a shot of Brian's whiskey.

Brian opened the door. "Hey, you're home early."

Mitchell dragged himself through the door and to the couch. Falling onto it, he threw his feet up on it and laid his head back on a pillow.

"This has been the worse fucking day of my life," he groaned.

"Whoa! What happened?" Brian sat on the coffee table next to him.

"Where's Sammi?" He wanted to hold Sammi in his arms, feel his lips press against his, to make Mitchell believe it had all been worth it.

"Around, I guess." Brian went to the back room. "Sammi?"

Mitchell closed his eyes and rubbed his temples. The pounding was still going strong, as if two jackhammers were busting concrete against the sides of his head.

Brian came back into the room. "He's not here. And all the stuff I bought him is gone, along with one pillow case."

"What?" Mitchell raised his head and stared at Brian. "Where'd he go?"

"I don't know, but he ruined a matching set of sheets." Brian's attempt at humor was met with a frown from Mitchell. "We had lunch, then I went to my office to get some work done. I left him out here watching TV."

"Shit." Mitchell swung his legs down and sat up. "After everything I've been through for him, I can't believe he took off." The air seemed to go from his lungs and he had to suck in a deep breath. His face twisted as he struggled to keep from falling apart.

"It's okay, man. Tell me what happened." Brian sat down at the other end of the sofa. "From the beginning. And this time, don't leave anything out."

Mitchell rubbed his hand over his face, sat back, and told Brian everything. About how he met Sammi, about their incredible connection, the break-in, Donovan, being fired, everything. When he ran out of steam and words, Mitchell closed his eyes and sighed.

Brian was silent for a long time. Mitchell waited for him to blast him about being a fool, about trusting strangers, about breaking his own rules, but it never came.

"First, we'll get your credit cards re-activated and re-issued. You'll be able to pick them up at the bank tomorrow. I have some money I can lend you until payday. You can worry about finding a job next week." He stood and got the phone. Then, he returned, sat on the couch, and held out his hand. "Hand over your wallet."

Mitchell passed it to him and listened as Brian dialed the number on the back, and explained what had happened. He passed the phone to Mitchell and he talked to the representative. By the time he hung up, she had guaranteed a new card would be waiting for him at the bank in the morning.

"God, I love you. Marry me," Mitchell told Brian.

"Not my type."

"I could dye my hair."

"Can you grow three inches and gain about twenty percent more muscle mass?"

"Maybe not."

"Besides, what about Sammi? You know, he knew something was wrong today. He told me he could feel that you were upset."

Mitchell looked at his best friend. "So you believe me? About the connection?"

"Yes. 'There are more things in heaven and hell than are dreamt of in your philosophy,'" Brian quoted.

"Thanks. Just makes me love you more." Mitchell smiled.

"Back at you. Now, we need to figure out what happened to Sammi. He left this morning, you know. He was gone when I came back from shopping. Said he went for a walk, but I'm not sure I believe him."

"It's possible, but the way he's been too frightened to go out, I doubt it. He's been terrified Donovan would find him."

"This guy Donovan. Any last name? Or is that his last name?"

"I'm not sure." Mitchell shrugged.

"Let me put in a call to some of my buddies on the force. See if they know anything about him."

"Why would they?"

"Just a hunch. When I finish, let's go over to your place, fix the front door, and I'll help you clean up." Brian gave his friend a grin and disappeared into his office, leaving Mitchell alone.

What would he have done without Brian? Friends like him came along maybe once in a lifetime. He'd been a rock of support when Steve had died, even listened when Mitchell had called at two o'clock in the morning to cry. Brian never made him feel like a whimpering, overly dramatic fag, but a man who'd lost the love of his life.

Now, Brian was there for Mitchell again.

If Sammi was supposed to be his soul mate, where the hell was he and why did he take off? Mitchell closed his eyes and opened himself, like he did when they made love.

Nothing. He was alone and a part of his soul had been ripped away. Mitchell felt empty, as if he'd been hollowed out with a spoon, his insides ragged and torn. The place in his heart that held Sammi was still there, but it ached.

Mitchell stood and went to the bedroom. Lying down on the bed, he pulled Sammi's pillow to his face and inhaled. Sammi's scent permeated it and filled his nostrils.

Sammi.

Chapter Nine

Sammi walked into the Laundromat and sat. A few people were doing their laundry, sitting around watching the television, reading newspapers or old magazines. He dropped his bag between his feet.

On the street again with no money. He knew what he could do to earn some cash, but he just couldn't bring himself to do it. And he didn't want to go to a bar and pick someone up. For the first time in his life, he didn't want anyone touching his body except Mitchell and he didn't want to touch anyone but Mitchell.

Across the street were several restaurants. Sammi stared at them through the glass window and chewed his thumb.

Picking up his pillowcase, he got up, walked out the door, and crossed the street. He went down an alley to the back door. It had been propped open with some boxes.

There was a man working in the kitchen, moving boxes around. Sammi stuck his head in the door and cleared his throat. "Excuse me, I'm looking for work. I can wash dishes or bus tables. Got anything?"

The man stopped and looked at him. "We're full up. Try next door."

Sammi nodded, went back down the alley to the street, around the front of the next restaurant and down the side. The door was shut, so he knocked. No answer. He knocked again and waited. Just as he was about to leave, the door opened and a head stuck out and spoke to him. "What do you want?"

"I'm looking for work. I can wash dishes, set and bus tables, anything."

For a moment, Sammi thought the man would tell him to get lost, but he gave Sammi a second look and then nodded. "Come on in."

Sammi followed him inside to a storeroom outside the kitchen.

"Take off the shirt and show me your arms."

Sammi obeyed. The old man searched his arms, then nodded. "Don't want any druggies. They steal. You steal, boy?"

"No, sir."

"Better not. I'll shoot you dead, you steal from me."

Sammi nodded, his eyes wide with fear. Maybe this wasn't such a good idea.

"Can you start now?"

"Yes, sir." Sammi's spirit soared. He never thought it would be this easy, just walk in, and ask.

"Good. Get that washer loaded. When you finish, I need the kitchen floor mopped." He motioned to the equipment with a scrawny arm.

"Yes, sir. Thank you, sir." Sammi grinned and rushed to the washer. Stacks of dirty dishes waited for him. He began to scrape off food into the garbage can and load the machine.

"Hey! You didn't ask how much I'm paying," the man called to him.

"Don't care." And he didn't. As long as he was off the streets and not selling himself, it didn't matter.

"I pay six dollars an hour, cash. I'll need you until we shut down at ten, maybe an hour after." On the street, before Donovan, Sammi had charged twenty for a five-minute blowjob. He had no idea how much Donovan had charged his upscale clients, but it was probably more money than Sammi had ever seen.

"Sounds good," Sammi called back as he rinsed a plate. He'd worry about where he was going to sleep later.

The man shook his head, grumbled, and got back to his boxes.

Sammi scraped off another dish, rinsed it, and stacked it. If Mitchell could see him now, he'd be proud of Sammi. But that was never going to happen. Sammi paused, blinked his eyes to clear the tears, and got back to work.

* * *

Mitchell leaned back and stretched. After a trip to the hardware store to buy a new doorframe and a better deadbolt, he and Brian had repaired the door. Now, his home was secure and he felt a little better.

They had bought a box of black plastic garbage bags and were going through the debris, saving what they could and throwing the rest away. Brian held the bag open as Mitchell dumped the contents of the sweeper into it.

"Think he came back to your place?" Mitchell asked.

"Maybe. If he does, he'll see the note you left."

"Think he'll wait?"

"Sure. Why not?"

Mitchell shrugged. He'd gone through the motions of cleaning like a robot, following Brian's quiet orders, not having to think about what he had to do. Brian always knew what to do.

They worked all afternoon and into the evening until the place was as clean as it had been before the break-in.

"Now, let's take a look at that computer of yours. I'll put some protection software on it and you're going to start using a password to log in," Brian told him.

"Yes, sir." Mitchell gave him a salute. "I feel like an idiot, leaving my info just sitting on the computer for anyone to look at."

"Don't. Lots of people do it."

After an hour of Brian's tinkering, Mitchell's computer was password protected and he'd gone into all the on-line programs Mitchell used to pay his bills and bank with and secured them.

They returned to the kitchen and sat at the table. Mitchell leaned back, pulled open the fridge, and took two Coronas from the door. After handing one to Brian, he twisted off the cap of his and drank.

"Cold beer. Gotta love it after a hard day's work." Brian raised his in a toast.

"Hits the spot," Mitchell said. He stared into space and let his mind drift.

Sammi.

Just as before, there was no answer.

"Hey, I'm starved. Let's go get dinner." Brian stood, drained his bottle, and tossed it in the trash.

"Can we swing by your house?" Mitchell looked up at his best friend. He stood and poured the rest of his beer down the drain.

"That was my plan." Brian slapped him on the back and they left.

* * *

Sammi gathered his pillowcase and stood at the back door of the restaurant. The man who'd hired him turned off the last of the lights. It was eleven-thirty. Sammi, covered in sweat, dishwater, and the smells from the kitchen, leaned in the doorway. He was tired, but it was a good feeling. He'd worked for honest pay for the first time in his life. It felt great.

"You did a good job, boy."

"Thank you, sir. What time tomorrow?" Sammi asked.

The man reached into his pocket and pulled out a roll of money. Licking his thumb, he counted out fifty dollars in assorted bills and handed it to Sammi. "Here's your pay. Can you come in at ten a.m.?"

"Sure," Sammi said.

They exited, and the man turned to lock up the door. Sammi walked to the sidewalk on Montrose and stood in the shadows between the buildings. He'd found a job. His next problem was where to sleep. He glanced across the street to the Laundromat and the sign that said "24 hours." He figured that was as good a place as any.

"You need a lift anywhere?" the man grumbled. He'd never given his name, and Sammi hadn't asked. For that matter, the old man had never asked for Sammi's name, either.

"No, sir." Sammi shook his head.

"Well, going to hang around here all night?"

"No, sir." Sammi pushed off the wall, slung his pillowcase over his shoulder, and dashed across the street and into the laundromat.

He found a seat and put his things on the chair next to him. Exhaustion flowed through him. He began to relax as he closed his eyes.

Moments later, the chair next to him creaked as someone sat in it.

"You plan on sleeping here tonight?"

Sammi cracked open an eye. It was his boss. "Yes, sir."

"Shit." His boss sighed. "Come on with me. I got a place off the avenue. You can bunk there for a few nights." He stood and waited.

Sammi nodded, picked up his stuff, and slung it over his shoulder. "Just the bed for a few nights? That's all?" He hoped the man didn't want anything else from him.

His boss looked at Sammi and grimaced. "What you think, boy? You think I'm one of those old perverts who like young—" He broke off and stared at Sammi. Then, he shook his head. "Just the bed, boy. I'm not going to touch you."

"Thank you, sir." Sammi gave him a curt nod.

"Come on." His boss left and Sammi trailed after him. As they walked down the avenue, he said, "What's your name, boy?"

"Sammi."

"I'm Otis."

They turned after two blocks and Otis walked up to what must have once been a two-story motel. Now, it housed low-income workers. They climbed the stairs, and Otis stopped at number nine and pulled out his keys.

Inside, Sammi looked around. One large room with a bed, dresser, couch, and TV. A small counter with a double cook top and a small refrigerator underneath. The only door was to the bathroom.

"You take the couch."

"Yes, sir." Sammi said. Otis tossed him a pillow and a thin blanket. Sammi arranged them as Otis went into the bathroom and shut the door. The shower ran for about ten minutes and then Otis came out dressed in his boxers.

"Bathroom's yours. Water will be hotter in the morning, but it's still warm now."

Sammi nodded and took his turn. As the warm water faded to tepid, he lathering quickly and then rinsed away the stink of the kitchen and his sweat. Using one of the thin white towels, he dried off and slipped into a pair of briefs. With the towel draped over his shoulders to cover his chest, he came out and crossed the room to his bed.

Otis was already asleep and snoring.

Sammi stretched out and pulled the blanket over him. Rolling onto his side, he remembered the feel of Mitchell's body against his. A perfect fit, unlike the couch. It poked and sagged, but it was good enough and Sammi was grateful for it.

In the morning, he'd get up and go to work.

Sammi smiled. Just like a regular guy.

* * *

Mitchell and Brian finished dinner and left the restaurant. Getting into Brian's SUV, Mitchell asked, "Can we cruise the avenue for a while?"

"Sure." Brian didn't ask why.

They drove up and then down the restaurant and bar studded avenue, and then up and down Westheimer for a few blocks. No Sammi.

Mitchell rode along, his eyes scanning the sidewalks for any sign of the man he'd known and loved. "Shit, Brian. What am I going to do?"

"Keep looking. Keep hoping he'll come back."

Mitchell sighed. "Maybe..." he didn't want to finish what he was going to say. It had been in the back of his mind all night. "Maybe it's for the best."

Brian was silent as he drove, watching the heavy traffic on all sides of his car.

"He's turned my life upside down."

"Yep."

"I lost my job because of him."

"Yep."

"My house was trashed because of him."

"Yep."

Mitchell glanced over at his best friend. Brian stared straight ahead.

"My life was threatened."

"Yep."

Mitchell sighed. "I've had the best sex of my life and I can feel again."

Brian didn't say a word, just kept driving, cruising along as Mitchell scanned the people walking in the night.

"I love him."

"I know."

"What the hell am I going to do?" Mitchell let his head fall against the seat's headrest. "What if he never comes back?"

"You'll go on. Let time heal you, just like it did with Steve."

They turned off the avenue and down Mitchell's street.

"Let's check your place first, then, for tonight, I think you should stay with me," Brian said. Mitchell gave him a grateful smile.

Brian pulled up and parked. Mitchell hopped out of the car and jogged up the steps. No note.

He came back down and got in. Slamming the car door shut, he said, "Let's go."

Brian drove off.

They got to Brian's and parked. The small porch was empty. The note Mitchell had left for Sammi was still stuck in the door where he'd left it. He pulled it out and crumpled it in his hand.

Brian unlocked the door and they entered. Mitchell walked to his room in a trance. "Good night, Brian."

"Night, Mitchell."

Mitchell shut the door, undressed, and then lay down. Pulling the covers over him, he floated on a dark sea with no light from the stars to guide him and no land in sight.

He should give it up and forget about Sammi. It was the best thing for both of them. He just didn't know how to let Sammi go.

Wherever Sammi was, Mitchell prayed he was safe.

Chapter Ten

Moretti scanned the club. Nothing but a bunch of old fags looking to hook up with young fags. He kept the sneer of disgust he felt from twisting his lips as he leaned over the bar and held out the photo of Sammi.

"Have you seen this guy?"

The bartender glanced at it. "No." His eyes took the bald man in and then sniffed. "Never seen him. He's cute. If you find him, I'd like to meet him." The bartender licked his lips and winked.

Moretti pulled the photo away and stuffed it back into his jacket. He'd lost track of the bars he'd been in tonight. Maybe his men were having better luck hitting the sex shops and video stores. As he moved through the packed club, his eyes darted from face to face, searching for his prey.

To his boss, the kid was money in the bank, just another body to sell on the market, funding the good life. Moretti knew Donovan had indulged himself with Sammi, just as he had with the women. Donovan swore Sammi had special abilities that made him valuable. For the life of him, Moretti couldn't understand what they could possibly be and he didn't care.

But the kid had caused all sorts of trouble for him, bringing Donovan's wrath down on him for letting him get away in the first place and for not being able to find him. Donovan just didn't understand the sheer number of fags that lived and played in Houston. They were like fucking roaches, coming out at night. For Moretti, the only way to treat a roach was to squish it.

A good roach was a dead roach.

Same with fags.

As he wound his way through the crowd around the bar, he made certain not to touch any of them. He didn't believe half of the crap on television, but AIDS was some scary shit and he wasn't sure if he believed that you only got it from butt-fucking, blood, and needles.

Moretti didn't indulge in daydreams often, but he had one where he'd beat the crap out of Sammi. He resented the fact that the little shit had escaped on his watch. It irked him, pissed him off, like a burr in his sock or an itch he needed to scratch, but couldn't reach.

Donovan had been quite clear, as soon as he'd recognized Sammi's talents, that Moretti not put a mark on him. And he never had, but he'd wanted to. Instead, he'd made the fag sweat. Workouts that lasted for hours, until Sammi's arms and legs shook. But, the little fag was as tough as his body had become and that had surprised Moretti.

Fags weren't supposed to be tough. They were supposed to be wimps, weak-wristed boy-girls who cried for their mamas. Sammi had never cried until Moretti realized that Sammi was terrified of confined spaces.

He'd taken real delight in preparing the closet. Pulled out the shelves, weather-stripped the frame, and installed the dead bolt. Nothing was getting out of that box.

When he finally caught Sammi, he hoped he'd find that bastard Collins, who'd been hiding him. Now, Moretti could hurt him. He hoped he'd catch them together, maybe fucking. That would be sweet. Moretti reached beneath his jacket and touched the holstered gun secured under his armpit. Oh, yeah, Collins would pay.

He finished his round of the club and left. The driver waited in the Mercedes at the curb. Moretti got in the passenger side and shut the door.

"Any sign?" the driver asked.

"No."

"Next place?"

"Let's try over on Westheimer. He hasn't been seen on Montrose in a week."

The car pulled away from the bar and cruised down the street, past closed restaurants, video salons, sex shops, and an all night laundromat. Moretti wondered who the hell would be doing his fucking laundry at two in the morning.

* * *

"Rise and shine, boy. Daylight's burning." Otis's rough voice woke Sammi.

He sat up, the thin blanket rumpled around his waist, and rubbed the sleep out of his eyes. Otis had dressed and was moving around in the miniscule kitchen.

"Morning, sir." Sammi rifled through his pillowcase and pulled out fresh clothes and the razor, but decided not to use up the aftershave. He wanted to save it for something special. Maybe if he ever got to see Mitchell again. Gathering it all up in his arms, he trod to the bathroom.

"Breakfast will be ready soon," Otis warned.

"Yes, sir," Sammi called from behind the bathroom door. He dressed and came out. "Can I help?"

"No. There's only room for one of us, and that's me. Got eggs and toast." Otis worked with a spatula, cooking the eggs in a small frying pan. The toast popped up from a two-slice toaster and he quickly pulled it out, buttered it, and put each slice on a plate. Then, he divided the eggs and slid them onto the plates.

Sammi took his plate and a fork and sat on the couch. Otis sat on the bed. They ate in silence with not even the TV on. When Sammi finished, he stood and took Otis's plate.

"You don't have to—" Otis began.

"I'm the dishwasher." Sammi's explanation seemed to satisfy Otis because he just gave a nod.

"It's eight o'clock. You don't have to be to work until ten."

"Don't have anywhere to go." Sammi shrugged.

Otis eyed him. Sammi dried the plates and forks with a towel. As he leaned over to return them to their places under the counter, he spotted a small mismatched collection of plates, bowls, and silverware all neatly stacked and organized. He carefully replaced the clean dishes.

Otis stood and made his bed. "Always believed if you live like an animal, you become like an animal."

Sammi went to the couch and folded the blanket. He placed the pillow on top of it and brought it to the open area where Otis's clothes hung. Above the pole was a shelf. Sammi stretched and placed his bedding on it.

Once the men had cleaned up, they sat on the couch. Otis picked up a section of newspaper, opened it, and began reading.

"Does the TV work?" Sammi asked.

"Yep. But I only get two channels clear and they're both Spanish. Can't understand a damn word," Otis grumbled. "Can you speak Spanish?"

"No, sir."

They sat in silence for a few minutes.

"Where'd you learn to cook?" Sammi asked.

"In the service. I was a cook in the Navy."

"Did you like being in the Navy?"

"Nope. But, at the time, it was the best I could do." Otis shrugged. "No education."

"I don't have an education either."

"I don't mean college, boy. I never finished high school." For reasons Sammi couldn't understand, Otis seemed proud of it.

"Neither did I." Unlike Otis, Sammi was ashamed of his lack of education.

"I dropped out, hung around my daddy's house until I was eighteen, and then enlisted just to get the hell out of there. They needed cooks and I figured you never hear of cooks getting killed, so I went for it."

"You were right. You didn't get killed." Sammi smiled.

"Nope. But I didn't like the ship. Too damn big and gray metal everywhere. For such big ships, they're small on the inside. Lots of small rooms. Lots of metal. Still don't understand how the hell the things stay afloat." Otis shook his head.

Brian could probably explain it since he had a college degree in engineering, but it was lost on Sammi too.

"I don't understand how planes fly, either," Sammi offered. "But they do, so I guess whether or not I understand doesn't matter."

"That's how I felt about the ships," Otis laughed and slapped Sammi on the back. "We got a lot in common, you and me."

Sammi wasn't so sure Otis would want much in common with him.

"You been on the streets before?" Otis asked.

"Yes, sir."

"You a whore?"

"Yes, sir, I was. Not anymore." Sammi chewed his thumb.

"Good." The old man nodded. "There's no future in it."

"No, sir."

"No future as a dishwasher."

"No, sir. But I don't intend to stay a dishwasher long."

"Well, got a little drive in you, huh?" Otis's eyes sparkled.

"I'm going to work my way up. Maybe be a chef." Until that moment, Sammi had never thought about what he wanted to be if he could be anything. He'd never thought about having a future that didn't involve sex.

"A chef! Not a cook, like me?" Otis teased him.

"First I'll have to be a cook. Then maybe I'll move up from there to a chef."

"Do you know the difference between a cook and a chef?" Otis leaned back and waited for Sammi's answer.

"No, sir."

"The size of the hat on their heads. Yes, sir, a cook has a little cap and a chef has a tall white hat, all pleated and fancy."

Sammi stared at Otis, who seemed to be holding his breath. When a smile crept onto Sammi's face, Otis burst out laughing. Sammi laughed along with him.

"You just wait," Sammi said. "I'll be wearing a fancy white hat before you know it."

"Not in my kitchen, you won't. Just little caps there. The boss don't pay enough money for a proper chef," Otis grumbled. "But I'll just bet, boy, one day, you'll wear one of those tall hats if you put your mind to it. You could go to one of those fancy chef schools where all they turn out is little food on big plates." The spark returned to Otis's eyes.

"I don't think I could get into a school like that." Sammi shook his head. "Will you teach me how to cook?"

"Let's get the dishes washed first. Then I'll see if I can get you moved up to help me in the kitchen. You got to do K.P. duty before you can swing a spatula."

Sammi smiled and nodded.

Otis turned on the TV and for the next hour, they watched Spanish programs that neither one of them understood, but they were so funny it kept both men laughing until it was time to go to work.

* * *

Donovan slammed his fist on the desk as he rose to his feet. "Son. Of. A. Bitch," he bit out. "If you tell me you can't find him tonight, I'm going to kill you. He has to be on that plane in two days."

Moretti stood in front of the desk and didn't say a word. His clothes reeked of cigarette smoke and cheap aftershave. Now he had to explain his failure once again.

"None of my men found anyone who'd seen him. It's like he's disappeared."

"I don't want to hear that!" Donovan shouted. "A half a million dollars. A fucking half mil. That's what I'm going to lose, all because of you."

Moretti didn't reply. No point.

Donovan took a deep breath and sat. Leaning back in the chair, Donovan stared at Moretti. Who the hell did Donovan think he was? Moretti had been with him from the beginning, when they were running a string of high-class call girls out of the most expensive hotels in Houston.

Then, Donovan got this idea about providing boys to rich men. At first, Moretti didn't think there was money in it, but he was surprised to find out how many old geezers wanted to fuck boys and pay very good money for it. Sammi had been Donovan's prize possession.

"You will find him tonight. No failures. Go to Collins. Lean on him, make him tell you where the little shit is. I don't care how many bones you have to break, but find the fucker." Donovan's voice had taken a dangerous tone.

"Right. It will be my pleasure." He gave his boss a nod and left, relieved to be out of there and not having to listen to Donovan's crap about his failures.

Signaling to one of his men in the hall outside the penthouse to join him, he pressed the button for the elevator and took his stance to the side of the doors.

No telling who could be there when the doors opened. Moretti might look dumb, but he wasn't stupid. He'd been an enforcer for too long to make stupid mistakes.

The bell dinged and the doors slid open. The old woman who owned the other penthouse got off with a little hairless dog in her arms. It barked at him as if it was going to attack and the woman gripped it even tighter. A gem-studded collar circled its scrawny neck. It reminded Moretti of a rat. From its big rat ears down to its long rat tail.

He hated rats almost as much as he hated fags.

If he ever got the dog alone, he was going to toss it over the fucking balcony. He liked that idea. Maybe he'd toss Collins over the balcony instead.

Chapter Eleven

Mitchell hadn't slept all night. Unshaven and bleary eyed, he sat at the table in Brian's kitchen, took a swig of coffee, and glanced at his best friend. Brian was a rock, solid and dependable. And dressed to kill. How did the man do it?

"What's your day like?" Mitchell asked.

"Well, I have an appointment with a new client this morning at eight thirty. Then I was going to catch up with some of my cop buddies and talk to them about this Donovan character." Mitchell poured his coffee into a mug that said "Firemen are Flaming Hot."

"I'd like to get the tires fixed on my car."

"How about after lunch? We'll take them to the tire place on Studemont."

"Sounds good."

"What are you going to do until then?" Brian watched him over his cup.

"Don't worry. I have no plans to sit around here and mope. I'm going walking." Mitchell said.

"You'll find him."

"Maybe."

Brian stood and gave Mitchell's shoulder a soft squeeze. "I think you will. I have a feeling." Then he scooped up his cell phone and keys, and he left.

It was seven a.m. when Mitchell left the house and walked to Montrose.

* * *

At seven fifteen, Moretti pulled up outside Mitchell's apartment and parked the Mercedes. He got out, went up the stairs, and pounded on the door. It had been fixed.

"Come on out, Collins!" he yelled.

After waiting a few minutes and pounding again, he decided either Collins wasn't in or he wasn't coming out. The neighborhood was waking up and people were starting to come and go. This was no time to kick in the door; one of the neighbors would be sure to call the cops.

Frustrated, he gave the door a final blow with his fist and decided to come back later.

* * *

By nine a.m. Mitchell had covered most of the strip. Without a photograph of Sammi, he had nothing but a verbal description to go by. The bars wouldn't be open until later that night, so he'd planned on hitting all the coffee shops, twenty-four hour video stores, and diners that were open.

There was only one positive I.D. and that was shaky. A guy in a coffee shop overheard Mitchell asking the waitress if she'd seen Sammi, and stopped him as he left. He'd said he'd seen a young man who fit the description, but it had been farther down the street, very late at night and he'd been walking with an old man.

Mitchell thanked him and put the info away for later. He intended to walk the strip that night, also.

Around ten a.m., he began canvassing the video stores. At the first one, he asked about Sammi and the clerk nodded.

"Yeah, man. Dude was in here last night. Had a photo of your boy, flashing it around. Told him same as you. I didn't see him." The guy shook his head. "And I don't want to see him with friends like that looking for him..." He shook his head again. "They some bad-ass dudes, man."

"Thanks. What size men are we talking about?" Mitchell wanted to confirm if Donovan's gorilla was searching in the same area.

"Hell, man, they was all big, you know? Scary, too." He sniffed. "You want to watch a movie with me? I got a free room in the back." He jerked his head to a black curtain that hung in a doorway.

"No, thanks." Mitchell left. If Donovan was still looking for Sammi last night that meant Sammi was still free, still out there.

The rest of the morning, Mitchell ran into more people who'd been asked about Sammi by what sounded like the same guys. Big, scary, and with photos of Sammi. Mitchell's gut told him there was something more going on than just a jilted lover.

Who was Donovan? From some of the descriptions the people gave, he must have at least four guys out looking for Sammi. Mitchell doubted they were good friends. More like paid muscle, if the guy who'd come to his work was any indication.

What Mitchell did know was that he needed to catch up to Sammi before Donovan or his men did.

* * *

Sammi and Otis trotted across the street and down the alley to the restaurant's back door. Otis unlocked the door and they went inside. Sammi began setting out all the clean dishes, wiping down tables, and filling salt and pepper shakers and ketchup bottles.

Otis had fired up the grill and fryer, and was prepping his work area. There were fresh tomatoes to cut, lettuce to wash and tear for salads, onions to chop, and lots and lots of potatoes to cut into fries.

Sammi kept his eye on the old man as he worked in hopes of picking up some idea of what a cook had to do before he even started to cook. At the penthouse, he often spent his free time in the kitchen, watching the housekeeper prepare their meals. Sammi looked forward to the time when Otis would let him do some prep work, but for now, he was content to wash dishes, clear tables, and do whatever was asked of him.

Today, he'd work enough hours to earn seventy-five dollars. With what he'd made yesterday, he'd have one hundred and twenty-five dollars. He hadn't had so much money in his pocket since he worked the street. Hoping he'd earn enough this week to rent a room somewhere, Sammi's spirits rose. The thought of staying at one of the shelters made him shudder. He'd been beaten several times at them, over stupid things like where his cot was, or that he had someone's blanket.

Without Mitchell, his life would never be complete, never happy. But maybe, for once, he could be proud of the life he did have.

* * *

Moretti decided to swing by Collins's place again. He'd called the fag's work number and had been told Mitchell Collins was no longer an employee, which almost made his day. Now he wanted to catch the bastard alone, lean on him, and find out where that little shit Sammi was hiding.

The car still sat on the street, tilting to one side from the two flat tires. Moretti grinned. It was a bitch to have one flat, but two? What a pain in the ass that had to be to fix. This time, he didn't bother getting out of the car; he just pulled over and parked. It looked like no one was home. Maybe the guy was out looking for work. Maybe he was wherever he had hid the kid.

Moretti waited another fifteen minutes, then drove off. He'd swing back this afternoon. Flipping his cell phone open, he checked in with his men. No one had gotten even a sniff of the little fag. He closed it and headed back to the penthouse to report in.

Donovan wasn't going to like it.

At this point, Moretti knew it would be sheer luck if he found Sammi. What he didn't know was if Sammi's good luck would finally fail, or if his own luck would finally kick in.

* * *

Mitchell and Brian met back at Brian's house. Mitchell opened a beer and downed it in two long pulls. Brian watched him, that odd look on his face, as if he knew something about Mitchell, but was trying to decide whether to say something.

"What?" Mitchell tossed the bottle in the trash.

"Nothing." Brian shrugged. "Are you ready to work on the tires?"

"Yeah, might as well. I need my car running so I can look for a job."

"Well, let's go. We can stop by your house and jack up one wheel, take it off and put on the spare, then take off the other one and get both fixed at the same time."

"Good idea. Do you think one of us should stay with the car?"

"No. I don't think anyone will bother it."

Brian's cell rang as they headed to the door. He unclipped it from his belt and answered. "Yep. Great. I'll meet you there around three. Thanks."

"Who was that?"

Brian locked the door and they got in the SUV. "One of my buddies on the force. He's got some info for me."

"Great. Maybe we can figure out who this guy is and why he wants Sammi so badly."

"I was wondering about that." Brian started the car and pulled out.

"This morning I found out Donovan's had several men out looking for Sammi. They have flyers, as if he were some lost kid," Mitchell grumbled.

"Well, makes sense. Sammi was with him for a long time. He'd have pictures of him."

"It's just strange. I'm searching for Sammi, but only because Donovan is, you know? I think if none of that shit had happened to me, if Sammi had just spent the night with me and left, I'm not sure I'd be looking for him right now."

"You'd just count it as love lost, right?" Brian asked.

"Yeah, right." He sighed and looked out the window. "I should stop."

"Stop looking or blaming yourself?" Brian gave him a look.

"Both, I guess. It's time I realized it's a lost cause. If Sammi wanted me, he'd be with me."

Brian glanced at Mitchell as they pulled up behind Mitchell's car. "Maybe he does, but for some reason you don't know about, he can't."

"Maybe," Mitchell said, as he got out, opened the Jetta's trunk, and retrieved the spare and the jack.

"You're still going out tonight to look for him, right?"

"Yeah." Mitchell gave a wry laugh. Brian knew him better than anyone in the entire world did. Except for Mitchell's mom. *Nobody knows you like your mother.*

Mitchell's mom had known he was gay before he knew it.

They changed the tires, brought them to the tire shop, waited for them to get fixed, then as three o'clock approached, Brian dropped Mitchell off with the tires.

"Look, I've got to make this meeting. I'll see you at my place at five. We'll have an early dinner and you can get back to the search," Brian said as he leaned over to talk to Mitchell out of the car window.

"That would be great. It's a date." Mitchell gave him a wave as he drove off.

It only took twenty minutes to get the tires back on. He stowed the jack in the trunk, and then hopped in the car and fired it up. He half-expected the car not to start or to explode like in the movies, but it started normally.

Mitchell pulled away and drove down to the park. He spent the rest of the afternoon cruising though Hermann Park, then back and forth on Montrose. At five, he went back to Brian's to meet him.

When six o'clock rolled around and Brian hadn't shown, Mitchell started the car. Flipping open his cell phone, he hit Brian's number and it rolled to the answering service. "Brian, it's me. I'm at your place. It's six. Sorry I missed you. See you later." He hung up and drove off.

At some point, he knew he'd have to give up the hunt for Sammi, but it wasn't going to be tonight.

* * *

Fucking roaches.

The dance floor seethed with men. Moretti weaved through them to the bar. He'd been in this place twice in the last week, but there was still a chance he might hit pay dirt.

At the bar, he motioned for one of the bartenders he'd never seen before. Holding out the photo of Sammi, he asked, "Seen him?"

The man took the photo, stared at it, and then shook his head. He handed it back to Moretti as if he were already bored. Turning around to face out into the club, Moretti steeled himself for another quick pass through the back tables, where couples sat holding hands, kissing, and giggling as if they were a bunch of schoolgirls.

It made him sick.

He'd pay Rhonda a visit tonight and fuck her brains out. Of all the whores he knew, he liked Rhonda the best. She could take it rough and that's how he liked it. Besides, it had been too long since he'd fucked and the time he spent around these fags just made him crave female companionship, if only for an hour.

Mitchell exited the bar and stood on the sidewalk. He'd been down both sides of Montrose and in a few blocks he would hit Westheimer. He'd have to go back to the parking lots of the club he'd left his car, if he wanted to drive. He felt as if he'd been walking all night and his feet were killing him.

He turned around and headed back to his car.

Sammi leaned against the door as Otis counted out the night's pay. The owner had given Otis the cash so he could pay his own help, since it was all under the table anyway. Stuffing the bills in the pocket of his jeans, Sammi waited as the old cook locked up. Then they walked down the alley to the street.

As he stepped onto the sidewalk, Sammi pulled his bandana lower on his forehead and put his head down. Someone might still recognize him on the strip.

Moretti exited the bar, shook himself like a dog throws off water, and stepped to the curb where the Mercedes was parked. The driver, Bert, sat behind the wheel waiting for him.

Mitchell looked up as two men came out of an alley. For a moment, Mitchell halted, staring at the tight ass in jeans as it walked away from him.

His heart skipped a beat.

"Sammi!" he yelled.

Moretti's head jerked up.

His eyes searched for the voice and found the man across the street, narrowed, then widened.

Shit. Mitchell Collins.

Collins raised his arm and waved at someone down the block.

Moretti's cold, merciless eyes tracked down the sidewalk. An old man stood next to a young dude with a bandana tied on his head. Son of a bitch, it was the fag.

He stepped away from the car, a smirk on his face. "Stay here, but be ready when I signal you." Bert nodded.

It seemed Moretti's good luck had just shown up.

Sammi froze. He should run but he couldn't make his feet move. Fists tight, he turned and his heart leapt into his throat cutting off his air.

Mitchell.

Sammi.

Taking a few tentative steps forward, Mitchell started toward Sammi. Letting Mitchell find him might be a mistake, but Sammi didn't care. Their eyes locked and Mitchell broke into a run.

Five feet away from Sammi, he came to a dead stop.

"Sammi. Where the hell have you been? I've been looking everywhere for you. Why did you leave?" Mitchell's words poured out as he gasped for breath.

"I had to go. I'd caused you so much trouble," Sammi's words stumbled out. The old man looked from one to the other and stepped back to give them privacy.

"Fuck that. I don't care about that." Mitchell's eyes were fierce, as if he'd face any fire. "I thought you knew that."

"I did, that's why I had to go." Sammi's eyes pleaded for understanding.

"Oh God, Sammi." Mitchell closed the gap between them and this time, Sammi met him halfway. They embraced with such force, Sammi's breath exploded out of him. Mitchell's warmth and love encompassed him, and Sammi melted against him. Resting his head on Mitchell's shoulder, Sammi looked at Otis.

"Go on, Otis. I'll catch up to you later."

"You sure, boy?" Otis eyed Mitchell.

"I'm sure, sir." Sammi smiled.

Otis gave him a nod and took off.

"Sammi." Mitchell stepped back into the shadowed alley, bringing Sammi with him. Sammi clung to Mitchell, unwilling to let go. He felt so safe in Mitchell's arms. Their separation had been a hell he'd had to endure and he never wanted to be apart again.

Mitchell jerked the bandana off Sammi's head. Burying his fingers in Sammi's hair, Mitchell tilted Sammi's head back and his mouth came down on Sammi's in a kiss that devoured him. Sammi met Mitchell's lips, mouth open and eager to taste his lover again.

Mitchell's tongue shot into Sammi's mouth, searching, touching, tasting. As Mitchell withdrew, Sammi sucked his tongue, pulling it back into his mouth, desperate to keep that sweet taste as long as possible. Mitchell moaned.

Sammi's back pressed against the wall of the building. Mitchell's hand stroked down Sammi's arm and their fingers entwined. Sammi's hand grabbed Mitchell's ass and pulled it toward him, grinding his stiff cock into Mitchell. For his part, Mitchell's rod, like a long, hard lump, dug into Sammi's belly.

This was where Sammi belonged. In this incredible man's arms.

"Well, well, well. Looks like my lucky day. I found two fags."

Moretti's oily voice froze the blood in Sammi's veins. Mitchell released him and spun around, placing his body in front of Sammi's to protect him.

"Get away from us, you bastard," Mitchell warned.

"Or you'll what? Cry?" Moretti smirked. He reached beneath his jacket and pulled a gun from under his arm.

Sammi's hands pressed against the brick wall. "Get out of the way, Mitchell," he whispered.

"Sammi doesn't want Donovan, can't you understand that?" Mitchell growled.

"Sammi doesn't have a choice and it seems you don't understand that." Moretti pushed the gun into Mitchell's belly with one hand and grabbed the back of his neck with the other. He leaned in and lowered his voice. "If you give me any trouble, I'm going to blow a hole in you big enough to walk through."

Mitchell froze.

"That's better. I think we understand each other. Now, we're going to get in the car and take a ride. All of us." Moretti pulled Mitchell around and held him by the arm, pressing the gun into his spine. "Sammi, if you don't want your girlfriend to die, you'll do as you're told."

"Yes, sir." Sammi nodded furiously. "I'm coming. Don't hurt him. Please."

Moretti signaled Bert. The Mercedes pulled to the curb as Moretti manhandled Mitchell to the car. He jerked open the door, shoved Mitchell in the back seat, and then opened the front door. "Get in the front, Sammi."

Sammi obeyed. Moretti closed the door and got into the back seat next to Mitchell, the gun pointed at his stomach.

"Bert, the penthouse," Moretti ordered. With a nod from the taciturn driver, the car pulled off and headed toward Westheimer.

Sammi sat in the front seat like a statue, too scared to move. His last meal rose in his stomach and afraid he'd puke, he swallowed and closed his eyes.

Donovan would not be happy.

Sammi would be punished.

Donovan would put him in the closet.

Tears filled Sammi's eyes and he blinked to stop them. He jerked his chin up.

Sammi would take the closet if it meant keeping Mitchell safe.

Chapter Twelve

Mitchell glanced down at the gun pointed at him. He'd never felt anything so terrifying as the cold metal of the gun pressed into his stomach. Now, his brain raced through all the possibilities that could happen to him and Sammi.

Donovan had to see reason. How could he make Sammi stay with him without doing anything short of kidnapping and holding him as a prisoner?

Mitchell had felt Sammi's fear. It had filled him in those moments when this gorilla had found them, but now it felt as if the tide of that fear had receded. Mitchell wasn't sure if that was good or not.

Mitchell didn't know much, but he understood his life was in jeopardy. He'd stumbled into something that he knew nothing about, but it involved Sammi and the man Donovan.

Drugs? He'd never seen any sign of drugs on Sammi.

Information? Certainly not computer info. Sammi seemed clueless about that sort of thing. But there were different types of info. Maybe Sammi knew something about Donovan that could ruin the man. Something he'd seen in the penthouse.

A murder? A surge of fear ran through Mitchell. Had Sammi been involved in a murder?

The car turned east on Westheimer and headed toward River Oaks, some of the most expensive real estate in Houston. Big money, big estates, big names. They turned at a high-rise glass building and followed the drive. With a sudden dip, the car plunged into a dark underground parking lot.

Bert parked the Mercedes in a numbered slot.

"We're going upstairs. No sudden movements. Bert, take Sammi," Moretti ordered.

"Sure, Moretti."

Now, at least, Mitchell knew the gorilla's name. Moretti. Sounded like a mafia hit man. Looked like one, too. Mitchell slid across the seat and got out of the car. Bert hopped out and trotted around the car, then pulled Sammi out by the arm.

Their small group headed toward the elevators. Mitchell led with Moretti behind him, the gun pressed into his back. Sammi and Bert walked side-by-side, Bert's hand on Sammi's shoulder. At the elevator, Bert pushed the button. Mitchell wondered if Bert's only job was to drive the car and push the elevator buttons.

The doors opened. Sammi hung back as Moretti and Mitchell got in. Mitchell wanted to say something to comfort Sammi, but he couldn't think of a word.

"Get in, Sammi." Bert pushed him forward. Sammi stepped over the threshold and closed his eyes.

Bert got in, turned, and of course, pushed the top button. It had a lighted capital P in the middle of the circle. They were going to the penthouse, just like Sammi had talked about.

The ride stopped and started as people got on and off. The men had moved to the rear of the elevator to give the other riders room. Moretti's gun, a steady pressure in Mitchell's back, was hidden from view.

After the twenty-first floor, no one else got on and they had the elevator to themselves.

"Donovan has missed you Sammi," Moretti said. "Did you miss him?"

Sammi's eyes had been closed ever since they'd gotten into the car, as if he were too frightened to open them. He stood silent and rigid against the opposite corner from Mitchell.

"Are you all right, Sammi?" Mitchell asked. He wanted to hold Sammi, give him some comfort, but there was no way Moretti was going to allow that to happen.

Sammi didn't answer. As if in slow motion, Sammi brought his thumb to his mouth and chewed on it. At least he could move.

After a soft ding, the doors opened. Across from the elevators was a large antique table with a fresh flower arrangement on it. Mitchell and Sammi were pushed toward the far side of the foyer to a door with a brass A it. At the other end of the foyer was another door that wore a brass B.

Moretti ran a card key through the lock. The light turned green and the lock clicked. He pushed down on the handle and opened the door.

Sammi swallowed his fear.

The burger he'd eaten for dinner rose in his throat again as his stomach rolled. He'd hoped to never come back here again, never see Donovan again. Hoped to escape being sold to another owner, forced to give his body to someone who used him like a possession, not a human being.

He'd been so stupid to think he could ever escape.

Walking to the center of the large room, he stopped. Donovan was nowhere in sight. He glanced toward the closed door to Donovan's office, then to the partially open door of his bedroom. He forced himself to look at the closet door. It floated on a long stretch of blank wall painted the color of a pumpkin. It looked so innocent, so harmless.

Just a door.

Sammi wondered if the door to hell was red.

His hell door was white and came with a deadbolt.

He turned his gaze to the wall of glass that looked out over the lights of Houston. When he'd first come to the penthouse, Sammi had been entranced by the view until it had become the only view of Houston he'd been allowed to see. His brief escape had only made his desire for freedom stronger, and the time he'd spent with Mitchell had given him only a taste of a life he'd never believed he could live. Of the man he never dreamed he could be.

Mitchell was pushed forward to stand next to him. Sammi fought to remain calm and keep his emotions reined in. The link between he and Mitchell was so strong that if he'd shut if off all of a sudden, Mitchell would have known it right away. Sammi had slowly been closing it and cutting himself off from the man he loved in a desperate attempt to shield him from Donovan's wrath. But something felt odd, a weakness grew within Sammi, sapping his strength as the link between he and Mitchell narrowed.

Life-force.

Their life-forces were entwined along with their bonded souls. He should have known, but like most of the things he knew about his power, he'd discovered them as he went. Otis had called that kind of learning hands-on training.

This was completely new and Sammi had no idea what was going to happen when Donovan put him on the plane to his new owner.

Would the separation kill him or Mitchell, or both of them?

"Sammi, are you all right?" Mitchell asked again.

Sammi chewed his thumb to keep from answering. Everything would depend on what happened when Donovan appeared.

"Sammi?" Mitchell's voice sounded as if he'd given up on reaching Sammi.

Good. Maybe Mitchell realized the danger he was in and would keep quiet and not cause any trouble.

Moretti crossed to the study and rapped on the door.

"Donovan. I found him."

There was a long moment where time and Sammi's heart stopped.

Then the door opened.

Mitchell's head turned as the man stepped out of the study. Dressed in a charcoal grey suit, he looked like an ordinary businessman. In an older man sort of way, he could even be called attractive. Frameless glasses highlighted icy blue eyes that held no warmth. Mitchell guessed his deep tan was sprayed on or from a tanning bed. However, Donovan's most striking feature was his thick, silver hair worn brushed straight back and long to just below his ears.

All in all, Mitchell could see what drew Sammi to Donovan. His wealth must have seemed like heaven to Sammi, who'd had so little. Donovan was clearly worldly and seductive, and that must have appealed to Sammi.

But Donovan couldn't hide the hardness around his mouth and coldness of his eyes. Mitchell could see the calculations Donovan made as the tightness around his mouth grew tighter and his cheeks tinted with the barest hint of pink.

Donovan was a dangerous man. And he was pissed.

"Sammi. Sweetheart. I'm so glad you've returned, although I'm not happy that I had to waste so much time and effort to find you." He approached Sammi and faced him.

Sammi didn't move a muscle, just stood still as Donovan stepped up, casting a shadow over Sammi's smaller body. Until Donovan had stood next to Sammi, Mitchell hadn't realized how big the man was. He wasn't bulky, but tall, and filled in, not lanky, somewhere between Mitchell and say, Brian.

Mitchell might have beaten Donovan in a fight, but Sammi, unless he knew karate or something like that, would have been out-sized and out-weighed. And neither of them could stand up against Moretti and his gun, so fighting their way out of this wasn't an option. Mitchell doubted that the odds hadn't been any better for Sammi before he ran away.

Reaching out a finger, Donovan stroked Sammi's cheek. Mitchell's abs clenched as he watched Donovan touch Sammi.

"As for you, Mr. Collins, I'm very unhappy with you. I asked for Sammi's return and you denied me. I don't like being denied what's mine."

"You talk like you have some sort of right to Sammi. He's not your property to buy and sell. He doesn't want to stay with you any longer, don't you get it?" Mitchell replied. Moretti moved to Mitchell's side, but the gun was holstered.

Donovan laughed. "I see Sammi has been up to his old tricks, haven't you, sweetheart?" He walked behind Sammi. Reaching over Sammi's shoulder, Donovan cupped Sammi's chin. "That was very naughty of you."

Donovan's cold eyes leveled at Mitchell. "I suppose you met in a bar. That's usually where Sammi picks up his marks."

Mitchell's eyes flicked to Sammi.

"Yes, well. Then, he told you what you wanted to do to him and I'm sure you wanted to do many things to my little Sammi." Another caress of his hand on Sammi's cheek. Mitchell couldn't stand it, but Sammi didn't flinch, didn't react to it at all.

"So we met in a bar, so what?" Mitchell shrugged.

"He used you, Collins, just like he'd used the other men he stayed with the other nights since he'd run away from me."

"What are you talking about?"

"That's what he does, Collins. He used those other men, just like he used you. To hide from me, because he knew I'd find him and make him come home."

Mitchell faced Sammi.

Sammi said, "Yes, I used you to hide from Donovan."

"Damn it, Sammi." Mitchell ran his hand over his face. "Why didn't you just tell me you were in trouble? I still would have protected you, no matter what."

Donovan laughed. "That's so noble of you, Collins. Really. But wasted on our little boy-toy."

Mitchell frowned and glared at Donovan.

"He's very good. Has the most extraordinary abilities when it comes to sex. I'm sure you've felt them? Did he know what you wanted or was thinking? Did he do all the right things to please you? Sammi knows how to use his powers, too. Did you know Sammi's been a whore since he was sixteen? He worked the streets until I found him and brought him here when he was twenty."

Mitchell's glare deepened.

"You're a whore, aren't you Sammi?" Donovan asked.

"Yes, sir."

"Say it, Sammi."

"I'm a whore."

"And the only thing he's good for is fucking," Donovan sneered.

"That's not true, you son of a bitch! Sammi. It's not true. You're more than what he tells you."

"Sammi belongs to me, Collins. He's mine."

"How can you say that? You don't own him." Mitchell's fist clenched. Moretti took a step closer.

"I do own him. From the top of his head to the tip of his perfect cock, I own him." Donovan stepped behind Sammi again. Wrapping his arms around Sammi, he tugged Sammi's T-shirt up to expose his belly and chest, and with the other hand, he teased Sammi's nipple. It pebbled in response.

"See? Sammi is trained to respond to sexual stimulation, no matter who it is. Sammi hates me, I promise you. But watch." His hand dipped down Sammi's belly and flicked open the button of his jeans. "He reacts. Like a trained dog."

Donovan ran his hand over Sammi's crotch. As Sammi's cock hardened, Mitchell jerked his head away and swallowed.

Sammi's eyes closed and he moaned. Damn, it was just like the sweet sounds he'd made when they'd made love. Mitchell couldn't stand it. The anger coiled in him.

"Stop it! Don't touch him!" Mitchell shouted.

"He's mine, Collins. Take my advice. Forget about him. Sammi's trouble." Donovan gave Moretti a tilt of his head and Moretti stepped up to Mitchell.

He didn't see the gorilla swing. Moretti's fist buried itself in Mitchell's stomach, forcing the air from his lungs. Mitchell groaned, doubled over, and clutched his belly.

Sammi groaned as his eyes flicked to Mitchell, bent over.

"I won't leave without Sammi." Mitchell grunted as he dragged air back in.

Moretti hit him again. Mitchell crumpled to the floor on one knee, bent over and gasping as pain radiated through his belly and chest. He'd been hit before in college, playing football, but this was different. The big, bald bastard had fists of steel.

Sammi groaned again and swayed as if he were going to faint but Donovan caught him in his arms to steady him.

Moretti laughed. "I've been waiting for this, you fucking faggot."

"I'm not a faggot," Mitchell bit out as he tried to stand. He hated that word and he used that anger to get to his feet.

Moretti hit him again as soon as he got upright, knocking him onto his back. Mitchell sprawled on the floor, stars shooting behind his eyelids.

"Give it up, Collins. Sammi is mine. Would you believe him if he told you?"

Mitchell rolled on his side and looked up at Sammi in Donovan's arms. He closed his eyes and opened himself to Sammi. There was nothing. It was gone. His connection, his bond with Sammi had been broken.

"Sammi. I can't feel you."

Sammi's eyes closed.

"Tell me you don't love me, Sammi. Tell me and I'll go." Mitchell rose to his hands and knees.

Sammi's eyes flickered and then opened. "I don't love you. I used you to hide from Donovan, but that was wrong. I see that now." He turned his head and lowered his voice as he spoke to Donovan. "If you let him go, don't hurt him, I won't give you any trouble anymore."

Donovan's eyes gleamed. "All right. Get him up, Moretti."

Moretti grabbed Mitchell by the front of his clothes and pulled him to his feet.

"Just one more." Moretti's arm cranked back and he slugged Mitchell in the face.

Mitchell's nose broke. Blood gushed, and ran down his chin and onto his shirt. The pain was stunning and he bled like a stuck pig. "Fuck you!" he shouted at Moretti, cradling his broken nose in his hands.

Sammi cried out. Moretti turned to look at him. "What the fuck?"

Donovan straightened. "What's going on? Did you hit him?

Blood streamed from Sammi's nose. He moaned, swayed on his feet, then collapsed.

Mitchell felt a wave of pain hit him and he reeled. Their bond returned and slammed into him like a Mack truck with Moretti behind the wheel.

Sammi lay on the floor in a growing pool of blood.

"Shit, no! You were right there. I never fucking touched him. He just started bleeding," Moretti yelled back.

Donovan's head swiveled back and forth between Mitchell and Sammi. His eyes widened. The horror and fear in them were clear as day.

"Son of a bitch!" He shook his head. "Moretti, whatever you do, don't touch Collins; just get him out of here. Take him back to his house."

He turned to Mitchell. "Sammi told you he used you. Now forget about him."

Moretti grabbed Mitchell as he started toward Sammi. "Oh, no you don't." He swung him around and marched him to the door. Bert, who'd been standing against the wall by the door, fell into step behind them, his eyes wide.

As the door opened, Mitchell twisted to get a last glimpse of Sammi. Donovan knelt next to him, holding a blood-soaked handkerchief to Sammi's nose. Then, the door shut and they were in the foyer. Bert rang the bell for the elevator. Moretti's grip on Mitchell's arm was like a vise.

What the hell had just happened? Mitchell had lost his bond with Sammi. There had been nothing and then it came back in a rush. He closed his eyes and faded.

Next thing he knew, they were in the elevator dropping to the garage level. He leaned back against the cool wall of the elevator to steady himself. Sammi had admitted he didn't love Mitchell and had just used him. It went against everything Mitchell had ever felt with Sammi, and he didn't know if he believed it or not, but damn it, Mitchell's heart felt as if it had been ripped from his chest. He wouldn't believe it. Could he have been fooled so easily? How could they have been so close and he not know it was all a lie?

Maybe Donovan was right and Sammi was an expert at using men like Mitchell, lonely and hungry for love, but he didn't want to believe it.

The doors opened and Moretti pushed Mitchell out. Mitchell stumbled, then caught himself. Moretti put a hand under his arm and moved him forward to the car.

Something wasn't right. That last glimpse of Sammi lying on the floor pushed through Mitchell's pain, as if he needed to remember something he was forgetting.

Sammi had collapsed at almost the same time as Mitchell, and Sammi's nose was broken and bleeding, just like his.

How could that happen? Mitchell's stomach did a flip as he realized the truth.

Sammi and he were not just soul mates. They were more. Somehow, in some way that he couldn't explain, their bodies and their lives were connected. Sammi had felt every blow Moretti had given Mitchell.

And if Mitchell knew that now, Sammi had known it before and had done what he did, and said what he'd said, in an effort to save Mitchell from Donovan.

Sammi had sacrificed himself to save Mitchell.

Chapter Thirteen

"Come on, Sammi. Stand up." Donovan pulled on Sammi's arm and helped him sit up. Blood was everywhere and the handkerchief Sammi held to his nose was solid red. "You've ruined the carpet, you know."

"Sorry, sir." Sammi got to his feet. Donovan helped him into the kitchen and to a chair. He fell into it as Donovan snatched the bloody cloth from him, tossed it in the sink, and gave him a wad of paper towels to use. Sammi almost told Donovan that he'd pay for cleaning the carpet, but he clamped his lips shut.

Donovan cursed as he looked down at his suit. "I need to get cleaned up, but first I'll get you some ice for your nose. I hope your eyes don't blacken."

"Me, too." Sammi knew Donovan's concern wasn't for him, but for his client. No one wanted damaged goods unless they were a bargain, and Sammi was sure Donovan wasn't selling him at rock-bottom prices.

Sammi stood, pulled off his shirt, and went to the sink to wash up.

He'd let the barrier drop when he'd seen and felt Mitchell being beaten and they had reconnected. That had been a mistake. If Mitchell thought there was any hope for

Sammi, he'd come back and if he did that, Sammi couldn't guarantee anything he did could save Mitchell.

Once Donovan put him in the closet, he wouldn't even be able to save himself.

* * *

Moretti pushed Mitchell into the car and he fell across the seat. The car started, they rushed through the garage, shot out of the tunnel like a rocket, and swerved onto Westheimer.

Closing his eyes, Mitchell leaned into the corner of the seat, a wad of his shirt held up to staunch the bleeding. The trip to his house was a painful blur.

The car pulled up and parked. Moretti reached across Mitchell, flung open the door, and with a shove ordered, "Get out."

Mitchell hurried out, bracing himself on the door. As Moretti pulled the door shut, Mitchell stumbled backward out of the way. The car sped off down the street and around the corner.

Digging into his pocket, Mitchell found his keys and climbed the stairs to his apartment. Once inside, he headed to the kitchen, pulled the shirt over his head, and tossed it on the floor, then ran the water at the sink.

He splashed warm water on his face. Watching as his blood swirled down the sink, he was reminded of the shower scene in the movie *Psycho*, only this was in glorious Technicolor. He grabbed paper towels and began to dry off his face. His nose still hurt but, thankfully, it wasn't swollen.

Mitchell got ice from the freezer, put it in a dishcloth, and held it to his nose. He pulled out a chair and sat. Reaching into the pocket of his jeans, he took out his cell phone, flipped it open, and punched in Brian's number.

This time he'd better be home.

* * *

Donovan reappeared in new clothes with a fresh shirt and jeans for Sammi to change into. He put them on the counter and leaned back against the doorframe.

"Change here."

Sammi stood and pulled his shirt over his head, then reached for the new shirt.

"No. Take your pants off first," Donovan ordered

Sammi frowned and bit his lip as he toed off his sneakers. The top button was already open, so he unzipped the jeans and shucked them off. He stood in the middle of the kitchen in his briefs.

Donovan's eyes roamed over his body. Sammi looked away. He'd seen that look so many times he didn't have to hear Donovan's thoughts to know what he wanted.

"Do you know what I want?" Donovan's voice sent a shiver down Sammi's spine as he approached. He was a dangerous man at the best of times and Sammi knew his mood could change in a heartbeat.

"A sandwich?" Sammi looked up at him.

Donovan's slap was fast and hard. Sammi's cheek reddened, but at least his nose didn't start bleeding. "Don't play the smart ass, sweetheart."

Sammi locked his lips and refused to open himself to Donovan, to read the man's most depraved thoughts.

"Take off your briefs."

Sammi hesitated, then did as he was told. Naked, fists clenched at his side, he stared back at Donovan, who was unbuckling his belt. The bulge in his pants had become pronounced. Sammi looked away.

"It seems you've picked up an attitude while you were on the streets." Donovan slipped his belt from the loops, hung it neatly on the back of a chair, and with one hand, flicked open the button on his trousers.

"I wasn't on the streets. I was living with Mitchell." Sammi's chin jerked up.

"You were fucking Mitchell for shelter." The zipper lowered, and he pushed his pants down and stepped free of them. After folding them over the chair, Donovan came closer to Sammi.

"No. I love Mitchell and he loves me."

"He used to love you, sweetheart. Now you've broken his heart and he's gone home to cry about it." Donovan's voice was syrupy sweet, but laced with bitterness.

Sammi refused to answer.

"You're a whore, Sammi. It's all you've ever been and all you will ever be."

"Not anymore." Sammi shook his head. For the first time in his life, he knew he could be more than what he'd been and he wasn't going back.

"You're my whore. I own you, Sammi. You're going to do what I say, and I say you're going to give me a blowjob. On your knees, sweetheart," Donovan growled.

"No." He'd never disobeyed Donovan before.

Donovan's eyes narrowed and he took a step closer, bringing him a hand span's distance from Sammi. Anger poured off Donovan. He'd either try to force Sammi to his knees or put him in the closet. If Sammi struggled, Donovan might hit him, but that would damage Sammi further.

It would be the closet.

A week ago, Sammi would never have believed he'd choose the closet over giving a blowjob but, right now, it was more important to Sammi to stand up for himself than take the easy way out on his knees.

"Get on your knees. Now!"

"No."

The front door slammed shut. Donovan grabbed his pants off the chair and slipped them on, then pulled on his shirt and stepped into his shoes.

"Boss?" Moretti called out from the other room.

"In here, Moretti," Donovan answered.

Moretti came in and stared at Sammi, then his eyes flicked to Donovan as he finished buttoning his shirt. "You need me?"

"Take Sammi to the closet. He needs to learn a lesson." Donovan glared at him.

Moretti grabbed Sammi's arm and jerked him around. Sammi stumbled, nearly falling, but Moretti held him up and marched him out of the kitchen, through the dining room, and into the living room.

Sammi's gaze fixed on the skyline of Houston. Thousands of shining lights filled the black expanse of the wall of windows.

Then they were in the pumpkin hall that led to the white hell door.

Moretti pushed Sammi against the wall and held him in place with a beefy arm across Sammi's throat. If he struggled, Moretti would merely lean harder and cut off more of the precious air Sammi needed. Sammi held still. Moretti unlocked the door, anked it open, grabbed Sammi by the back of the neck, and pushed him toward the narrow opening.

Sammi's heels dug in as he strained backward. He'd known all along it would come down to this moment, but he was still terrified. Not of going in, but what would happen once the door closed, shutting out all the light and sound in that too-small space.

Telling himself it was worth it to keep Mitchell safe, Sammi unlocked his knees and with a final heave, Moretti tossed him inside.

Sammi hit the wall of the closet and spun around in time to see the grin on Moretti's face as he slammed the door shut, bathing Sammi in cool darkness.

The dead bolt slid into place with a soft snick.

Sammi was alone in the dark.

* * *

The furious banging on the front door brought Mitchell awake. He sat up on the couch and pushed to his feet. Opening the door, he let Brian in.

"What the hell is going on?" Brian, like a whirlwind, blew past him and into the house.

"Like I told you on the phone. Donovan has Sammi and that bastard Moretti beat me up, then dumped me back here." Mitchell went back to the couch and sat.

Brian's fists were white knuckled as he sat on the coffee table across from Mitchell. "Let me see."

Mitchell lowered the ice pack and Brian's worried blue eyes searched his face, assessing the damage as one hand rested with a comforting weight on Mitchell's knee.

Brian gave his decision. "He broke it."

"I know that."

"It's not bad. It looks pretty straight." Brian took the ice pack and replaced it gently against Mitchell's nose.

Mitchell smiled. "Thanks. Are you sure you won't marry me?"

"I told you, you're not my type."

"Ok, but if we get to forty and we're still alone, then will you marry me?" Mitchell grinned.

"Okay. But I'm cooking." Brian nodded.

"Deal." Mitchell laughed. They both knew Mitchell couldn't cook worth a shit and they both knew they'd never screw up their relationship by becoming partners.

"Now, tell me everything that happened at the penthouse." Brian moved to the couch to listen as Mitchell told him in detail as much as he could remember.

Brian didn't respond, just listened intently until Mitchell had finished.

"So, Sammi's nose started to bleed when yours did?" Brian asked.

"Right. And I'd swear he felt those punches," Mitchell insisted.

Brian sat back, closed his eyes, and chewed the corner of his lip as he thought, then let out a breath. "Here's what I know. I didn't meet you yesterday because I caught up with the vice cop I know. When I mentioned Donovan's name, Pete went berserk. Seems they've had their eye on him for years, but have never been able to prove anything."

"Vice? Like prostitution?"

"No. Worse." Brian reached out and touched Mitchell's leg. "Mitchell. Sammi is a sex slave."

Mitchell stared at his best friend and the room shrank to Brian's face. "What the hell are you talking about?"

"After talking to Pete, I believe Sammi is a sex slave. Usually they're people who have fallen between the cracks, or are living illegally in the country with no resources, no families. They get picked up off the streets by sharks like Donovan. Now, they may already be into prostitution or maybe not, but once these guys get hold of them, they take control. Steal their papers, if they have any, or take all their money and lock them up. Then, these people are sold to the highest bidder, usually on the Internet."

"And you think that's what happened to Sammi?"

"Yes. His history is perfect for it. Lost in the system and fallen between the cracks. Did he ever give you a last name?"

"No. But I never asked." Mitchell looked at his feet then up into Brian's face. "I have to go back, Brian. I have to get Sammi out of there."

Brian shook his head. "It's too dangerous. Moretti is an experienced gun and from what Pete told me, he and Donovan have been in the business for a long time. They aren't amateurs."

"I don't care what you say, I'm going back." Mitchell stood and looked at the ice pack. His nose felt better and had stopped bleeding. "Are you coming or do I go by myself?"

Brian stood and faced him. "Do you have a gun?" The look on his face was dead serious.

"You know I don't."

"I brought one for you in the car."

Mitchell gave a dry laugh. "You knew it, didn't you? You knew I'd want to go back and get Sammi."

"It's what I'd do if someone was holding the man I loved."

"Thank you." Mitchell held his arms out and Brian slipped into them. They embraced and then Brian slapped him on the back.

"Let's go. Pete and his men are going to join us when we pay Donovan a visit."

"You talked the cops into helping?" Mitchell stared at him.

"Couldn't keep them out of it. It's a big bust. They're getting a warrant for the penthouse right now. We'll just be there to get Sammi. We're background, Mitchell. That gun stays in your pocket, get it?"

"Got it." Mitchell went to his room, got his jacket, and put it on. He was ready to go by the time he got to the front door where Brian waited for him.

They left and got into Brian's SUV. Brian reached around, picked up a small gun, and handed it to Mitchell. "It's my backup weapon. I use it in a holster that I wear at the small of my back, but you're going to put it in your pocket. Don't touch it and keep it out of sight." Mitchell had known Brian had a gun. In his line of work, he had to. It could be a matter of life and death, but Brian had never really talked about it. Mitchell felt out of step with his best friend but it came with a whole new slice of respect.

"Well, if I'm not supposed to use it, what do I have it for?"

"I didn't say not to use it, did I? Just keep it out of sight around the cops. It's a lot easier to ask forgiveness after than permission before." Brian gave him a wicked grin and they pulled away from Mitchell's house.

"Where's your gun?" Mitchell asked. This was so weird. He felt as if he and Brian were some sort of film noir private eyes on a case.

"Shoulder holster."

"Aren't these concealed weapons?"

"Yes, but I'm licensed to carry. You're not. Hence, the stealth."

Mitchell nodded and watched out the windshield as they approached the high-rise. They pulled into the garage and parked in a visitor spot next to a large white van.

They got out and Brian walked over to the van. The door opened and a cop got out and shook his hand.

"This is Pete. Pete, this is Mitchell Collins. It's his friend who's being held against his will upstairs."

Pete, a man built like a tank, low to the ground but powerful, nodded to Mitchell.

"Has Brian filled you in?"

"He said you have a warrant," Mitchell said.

"That's right." He held up a paper. "Search and seize."

"I just want Sammi free. He won't be arrested, will he?" Mitchell looked from Pete to Brian for assurance. This would be for nothing if Sammi was arrested and jailed. The idea of Mitchell being the cause of relocating Sammi from one prison to another turned his stomach. He'd wanted to free Sammi, not send him to jail.

"Sammi should be fine. We'll need his testimony against Donovan and Moretti. Yours too, in the assault," Pete said.

"You got it. I'll do anything to put those two bastards where they can't do this to anyone again." Mitchell frowned and touched his nose. Still tender, he winced and then dropped his hand to his jacket pocket. The gun hidden there felt very heavy and he wasn't sure he liked carrying it at all, despite the image of hard-boiled P.I. it evoked.

Pete opened the back of the van, and several cops dressed in black with bulletproof vests that said HPD filed out and joined them. After several quiet conversations, the group headed to the elevator.

* * *

Absolute darkness.

The walls touched his bare skin. Sammi shivered and licked his lips. Telling himself that he could do this, that time would pass quickly, he inched forward to stand in the middle of the closet.

Sammi inhaled, counted to ten, then exhaled. He repeated the exercise, using it to steady himself and to insure he didn't hyperventilate. Last time he'd done that, he'd passed out only to awaken slumped on the floor of the closet, touching the sides, feeling how very close they were to him.

Which started the cycle all over again.

Closing his eyes, he could pretend the walls were far away and there was plenty of room around his body.

No need to panic. Everything was fine. Donovan would let him out soon.

Control was necessary, but fleeting. He'd never been able to keep control, sustain the image of a larger space. This time, he would do it.

The weakness returned. Sammi swayed in the dark. He opened his eyes. Darkness surrounded him. The walls were closer than before and it was harder to breathe.

Sammi lost count of his breathing. Shaking, he began again, inhaling, counting, exhaling. Five times. Ten times.

Twenty times.

The walls were definitely closer. He was going to use up all the air in the closet if he kept breathing like this but, if he didn't breathe, he'd panic.

His next inhale was ragged. He struggled to pull enough air into his lungs. Dizzy, he began to fall, and reached out a hand to stop himself. It slammed into the wall and his fingers bent back. Sammi cried out in pain.

His voice boomed and echoed. Sammi reeled, falling back. His shoulder touched the wall and he gasped. Spinning around, Sammi tried to get back into the center, back to the safe spot, back to breathing as if each breath were his last.

He was losing it.

Sammi opened himself.

Mitchell.

In the elevator, Mitchell felt the elevator tip sideways. His throat tightened and he sucked in a deep breath. Next to him, Brian turned to him.

"Mitchell. What's wrong?"

"I can't breathe." Mitchell clawed at his throat, gasping for air. The elevator was too crowded, too many men, not enough space.

Mitchell lurched forward and the cops around him stepped back.

"What the hell's wrong with him?" Pete said.

"I don't know." Brian shook his head and grabbed Mitchell's arm.

Fear poured into Mitchell and he broke out into a sweat, coating his forehead, upper lip, drenching his underarms. Desperate, his eyes darted around the elevator cabin.

"I have to get out," Mitchell groaned and pushed forward past the men in front of him. His fingers clawed at the buttons, hitting several of them.

The elevator stopped and the doors opened on floor seventeen. Mitchell broke free with Brian on his heels. Pete stood in the door, holding the elevator.

Brian grabbed Mitchell's arm. "What's going on?"

"It's Sammi. He's in the closet. They put him in the closet," Mitchell whispered.

Brian leaned closer to hear him. "You can feel it."

"I'm feeling what he's feeling." Mitchell knew it sounded wild, but if anyone would believe him, it was Brian.

"Right. Listen to me, Mitchell. You have to help Sammi. You have to help him calm down. You're not claustrophobic, so you can rise above this fear. Help him." Brian looked deep into Mitchell's eyes.

Mitchell nodded. Closing his eyes, he steadied himself and reached for a calm spot in his mind. His breathing slowed and the panic dispersed. Then, he pushed outward, searching for Sammi.

Sammi's breathing eased as a feeling of well-being and calm filled him. In the next heartbeat, he knew he'd reached Mitchell and that Mitchell was giving him this gift of calm, sharing his peace of mind, pushing Sammi's fear from the dark corners of the closet he was trapped in.

If that was true, then Mitchell was coming back for him.

No one had ever come back for him. Tears filled his eyes. He was torn between his need for Mitchell and wanting to keep the man he loved safe. But locked in this closet, Sammi wasn't much good to anyone.

Slowly, Sammi lowered himself to the floor, his hands touching the walls he once feared. He crossed his legs and sat. He could breathe easier now. With Mitchell's help, he could survive.

Mitchell followed Brian onto the elevator and Pete let the doors go. They arrived at the top floor a few minutes later. The cops poured out of the cabin and spread out, flanking the door to apartment A. Brian and Mitchell stood back behind the officers.

"Remember, this is their show," Brian said. Mitchell nodded, concentrating on sending Sammi soothing feelings. From the response he felt from Sammi, it was working.

Pete knocked on the door and stepped to the side.

Mitchell waited and held his breath. A flutter in the bond between him and Sammi brought him back. He exhaled and took up his regular breathing. The bond smoothed out.

The door opened. Moretti took one look and threw his weight against the door to keep them out.

"Police! Open up! We have a warrant to search the premise," Pete shouted.

Two cops on either side of the door used their shoulders to force it open, throwing Moretti back. The rest of the men swarmed through.

Brian and Mitchell were the last ones to enter the penthouse.

Donovan came out of his study. "What's going on?" With one look at the cops, he turned and raced back through the door, but one of the cops was quicker.

"Get his computer! Don't let him touch it!" Pete shouted. The cop caught Donovan, pushed him to the floor, and cuffed him.

It took two cops to hold Moretti against the wall as another searched him. They found the gun immediately. "He's carrying," the cop told Pete.

"I got a license to carry that," Moretti growled.

"We'll check into that later at the station. For now, you'll wear these cuffs for your own safety." With a quick twist of his arm, the cop had Moretti's wrists bound and began to read him his rights.

"Is that everybody?" Pete asked, his head swiveling around. "Where is your friend?"

Mitchell strode into the middle of the room.

Sammi.

Mitchell.

Rushing to the hall, Mitchell found the lone door. He tried the knob, it turned, but the door wouldn't open. Shit. There was a deadbolt above the knob. He unlocked it and opened the door. The closet was empty.

"Sammi?"

"Mitchell." Sammi's soft voice came from below him.

Looking down, Mitchell found Sammi, naked, curled up on the floor of the closet, his hands over his eyes to block the blast of light from the hall.

"You're a sight for sore eyes." Mitchell sighed. Aware of all the cops around him, he refrained from pulling Sammi into his arms and kissing him. "Wait here. I'll get your clothes."

"They're in the kitchen, I think." Sammi said as he sat up, blinking, and saw the cops staring at him. One hand covered his genitals; he held the other over his eyes.

Brian crouched down to Sammi. "How're you doing?"

"Fine." Sammi lowered his voice so only Brian could hear. "Mitchell helped me stay calm."

"I know." Brian winked at Sammi, then stood as Mitchell returned.

Sammi took the jeans Mitchell held out and pulled them on. He stood and zipped them up, then Mitchell handed him a fresh shirt. Sammi leaned against the wall as he put it on.

With Brian leading and Mitchell at his side, Sammi walked into the front room a free man.

"I'm going to get you for this, you little bitch!" Donovan shouted. Sammi flinched, but Mitchell placed his hand on the center of Sammi's back to steady him.

Moretti, hustled by a cop on each side, glared at Sammi, then disappeared through the door. Pete gave a few last orders to some of his men, and led Donovan, shouting for his lawyer, out of the penthouse.

"Let's go. There's nothing for us to do." Brian motioned to the door.

"Can I take my clothes?" Sammi asked, pointing to his room.

"I'll check." Brian motioned to one of the officers. "Is it all right if he takes his clothes?"

"Sure. Just the clothes and you'll have to give your statements before you leave."

Mitchell sighed, and Sammi nodded as the officer pulled out a pad and began asking questions.

Chapter Fourteen

Mitchell, Sammi, and Brian finished dinner. Sammi insisted on doing the dishes and sent the two men out of the kitchen to the living room.

Mitchell sat on the couch and Brian took the chair across from him.

"How's he settling in?" Brian's eyes darted toward the kitchen. It had been almost a week since they'd freed Sammi from Donovan.

"Fine. He's still a little shy about going out, but he's getting better," Mitchell replied.

"It takes time. How are things between you two?" Brian raised an eyebrow.

"Well, if you mean our bond, it's as strong as ever. If you mean the sex, it's phenomenal." Mitchell couldn't help but grin.

Sammi joined them and sat on the couch next to Mitchell. Sliding under Mitchell's arm to snuggle against his chest, Sammi was right where he belonged.

"I have a couple of things I want to discuss with you, Sammi," Brian said.

"With me?" Sammi glanced at Mitchell, but Mitchell just shrugged. "Okay."

"I talked to Pete. The D.A. thinks the conviction is in the bag. With your testimony and with all the evidence they found on Donovan's computer, he's going to be locked up for a very long time. Maybe life."

"That's good to know." Sammi exhaled. What a relief. He still half-expected to see Donovan or Moretti around every corner.

"Pete's a good friend. He understands a lot of things. So, I wasn't surprised when he gave me this." Brian leaned forward, picked up a large brown envelope from the coffee table, and handed it to Sammi. "These are yours. There are no copies."

Sammi looked at Mitchell, then opened the folder and slid out a dozen photographs. The blood rushed to his face as he shuffled through them while Mitchell watched. They were Donovan's photos of him, naked, in a series of erotic poses.

He shoved them back into the folder and clutched it in his hands.

"It's not my business," Brian said, "but if I were you, I'd burn those when I got home tonight."

"Burn them?" Sammi asked.

Brian sighed. "Sammi, you're young. You have a new future ahead of you, one where photos like this might become a serious problem. Burn them."

Sammi nodded; he wasn't sure about the future he had ahead, but he didn't voice his doubts. He slid the envelope onto the table and sat back. Mitchell gave him a reassuring hug as he pulled Sammi to his side.

"What's the other thing?" Mitchell asked.

"Let's have a drink," Brian said, then stood and went to his bar. Taking down three short crystal glasses, he uncorked the decanter, poured three whiskeys, and returned.

Sammi took the glass and looked down into it. "What's this?"

"Whiskey. Time to put some hair on your chest," Brian drawled.

Sammi frowned and took a big sip. He gasped as the dark liquid burned its way down his throat, filling his head with its vapors. Trying not to cough, he choked instead.

Mitchell and Brian laughed. "Got to sip it, babe," Mitchell said.

Sammi nodded and tried again. A little sip wasn't so bad. It still burned going down, but in a warm, sexy way. "It's better."

Mitchell's hand caressed Sammi's leg, offering reassurance. Sammi was safe with these two wonderful men. How had this happened to him? He didn't deserve any of this, and yet it had happened. Mitchell had come into his life and turned it upside down, like a trailer after a Texas twister.

Upside down felt fantastic.

Brian leaned forward and rested his elbows on his knees. He held his glass between his hands and slowly rolled it from side to side. Sammi watched, as Brian seemed to gather himself for what he had to say.

Butterflies danced in Sammi's stomach.

"You know I'm a P.I., right?"

Sammi nodded.

"I do all sorts of work. One of the things I do is track people down, find out where they are. Sometimes, I find out *who* they are." Brian's eyes bored into Sammi's so intently that Sammi didn't want to say a word would that might break the spell.

"I believe I can find out who you are, Sammi."

Sammi's glass slipped from his hands and hit the wood floor. It didn't break, but what was left of his whiskey spilled. "Sorry," Sammi stuttered and reached for the glass.

Mitchell put out a hand to stop him and pulled Sammi back to his side. "Later."

Sammi focused on Brian. "You can find out my real name?"

"I think so. And once I have your name, we can locate your birth certificate."

Sammi's mouth dropped open and he spun to face Mitchell, searching for confirmation.

"With a birth certificate, you can apply for a social security card. Be a real person, with a future and countless opportunities," Mitchell said.

Sammi swallowed and tears welled in his eyes. He really wished he had that whiskey back. He reached over, snatched Mitchell's glass, and downed it.

Coughing, eyes running, Sammi laughed, then jumped up and fell onto Brian.

"Thanks, Brian. You're the best friend I've ever had," Sammi gushed. "Other than Mitchell," he quickly added.

Other than Otis, Brian was Sammi's only other friend, but he didn't need to point that out.

Brian wound up with Sammi in his lap. "Hey, now. Real men don't jump into other real men's laps. It's against the code." Brian's face took on a pink flush.

Sammi laughed. "You're blushing."

Mitchell laughed. "Sammi, not even our tougher-than-nails Brian can resist a man as beautiful as you. Even if you aren't his type."

Sammi frowned. He almost asked what Mitchell was talking about, when he felt Brian's hard reaction to him sitting in his lap. "Oops!" Hopping off, he grimaced. "Sorry."

"No need to be sorry." Brian shook his head. "Sexy as hell."

"And nothing but trouble," Mitchell finished.

Sammi slid next to Mitchell. "I thought you liked sexy." He looked up from under his bangs into Mitchell's eyes.

"I do, but I love trouble, too." Mitchell pulled Sammi on top of his lap.

Sammi wrapped his arms around Mitchell's neck, lowered his mouth, and kissed him. He tasted the heady whiskey on Mitchell's sweet tongue and moaned. Mitchell joined him in that soft sound as their kiss deepened.

"Get a room!" Brian laughed.

* * *

Today, Mitchell had gone on an interview. This was his third call back for a position at another oil company. Mitchell would hear this morning if he got the job.

Sammi sat in the kitchen, chewing his thumb as he waited for Mitchell to come home. Over the last two weeks, Sammi had spent most mornings experimenting with breakfast and lunch, cleaning the apartment, watching television, and taking walks with Mitchell around the neighborhood. A small coffee shop located off the avenue had become their favorite destination.

All that time, Mitchell had assured Sammi that his finances were good, and that he would have plenty of money once his last paycheck had been deposited, but Sammi still felt bad that he wasn't pulling his weight.

When Brian found out who he was, that would change. However, Brian had warned him that it might take some time, maybe even a few months. Sammi knew Brian had other paying work to do, so Sammi was determined to be patient.

But his patience extended only to himself. Mitchell had been gone since eight thirty for a nine o'clock appointment and now it was after twelve.

The front door opened. Sammi stopped gnawing on his thumb and opened himself to Mitchell. Other than the connection between them, humming like a high-voltage wire, Sammi got nothing.

Sammi smiled. Mitchell had become good at blocking as he tested his own power.

"Sammi!" Mitchell called out from the hall.

"In the kitchen," Sammi called back.

Mitchell came in, a large bag in his hand which he put on a chair. Sammi watched his face for any signs of the results of his interview, but his stoic expression told Sammi that Mitchell was enjoying himself.

"Mitchell! What happened?" Sammi couldn't wait any longer.

"I got the job." Mitchell's face broke into a magnificent grin.

Sammi jumped up and threw his arms around Mitchell. "I knew it. I'm so proud of you." He kissed Mitchell and melted into the man's arms. Mitchell kissed him soundly, then took Sammi by the arms and pushed him away.

"I have something for you."

"A present?" Sammi's eyes widened. He loved getting presents and Mitchell loved giving them. One day, Sammi would have enough money to give Mitchell many fine gifts.

"Only if you accept it." Mitchell leaned over and picked up the bag. "Sit down, babe."

Sammi sat back in his chair, his hands clenched together on the tabletop. His knee bounced wildly beneath the table. "What is it?"

Mitchell pulled the bag away and placed a huge book in front of Sammi.

Sammi stared at it. It was almost three inches thick and bigger than any book he'd ever touched. He scanned the title. "What's GED?"

"That's G-E-D. It stands for General Education Degree. Basically, it's like a high school diploma." Mitchell touched the book, pointing out the words.

"What's it for?" Sammi stared at the book, then up into Mitchell's face.

"Sammi. If you study this book, I'll bet in six months you could take the test, pass it, and earn your high school diploma."

Sammi looked down at the book. "Four years of high school in this one book?" His eyes widened and he shook his head. "I'm not that smart, Mitchell."

Mitchell's hand slammed down on the table and Sammi jumped. "Don't ever say that, Sammi. Don't ever sell yourself short. You're smarter than hell. You had to be to survive on the street and that bastard Donovan." His voice was so strong, so adamant, that Sammi couldn't help but believe him.

"Six months?" he asked.

"Maybe faster if you work hard." Mitchell nodded.

Sammi opened the book and began to read the first page. Mitchell laughed, and reached out to lay his hand over Sammi's. "One more thing, babe. Well, a couple, really."

"What?"

"I spoke to Otis this morning. He wants you back. He told me you're the best worker he's ever had and he was looking forward to passing on his skills as a cook to you."

Sammi sat up. "Otis wants me back?"

"You never told me you wanted to be a chef." Mitchell's voice was soft and Sammi wondered if he'd hurt Mitchell by not sharing that, but when Donovan had taken him off the street that night, he'd given up on that dream.

Sammi shrugged. "It's silly, I know."

Mitchell's voice hardened. "Don't say that. It's not silly. It's good. Something you can be proud of. You start with Otis on Monday. He said to be there at ten."

Sammi's head reeled. A high school diploma and a job. It was too much. Never had so many good things happened to him. He nodded. "I'll be there."

"Good. I was thinking, after you get your G.E.D. if you'd like to enroll in college in the fall, I could help you with that."

"College!" Sammi bolted to his feet. "I can't—" At the look of warning in Mitchell's eyes, Sammi cut himself off. Mitchell was right; no more negative talk.

"I never, in my wildest dreams, ever thought I'd go to college."

"The University of Houston has an amazing culinary program. You can work at Otis's until fall and earn money for the tuition, and I'll help you with anything else you need," Mitchell said. "But only if you *want* to go to college."

Sammi looked down at the book that held his future. A future he never would have had without this man. Mitchell had given him so much more than he thought he'd ever have.

Looking up, Sammi let the tears spill down his cheeks. "I knew you loved me, Mitchell. But I never thought you believed in me."

Mitchell opened his arms and Sammi went to him. Resting his head against Mitchell's shoulder, Sammi took all the love and strength Mitchell offered him.

Sammi was a free man, but Mitchell had captured Sammi's heart and soul.

Mitchell whispered into Sammi's hair. "Bedroom. Now. If I can't touch your skin soon, it's going to kill me."

Chapter Fifteen

They raced to the bedroom. Sammi made it there first, with Mitchell a close second. Mitchell won the race to get undressed and fell onto the bed. His cock, already hard, stood proudly from his body.

Sammi sighed as he just stared at Mitchell. "You are so beautiful."

Mitchell laughed.

"But something isn't right." Sammi shook his head.

Mitchell's smile fell. "What are you talking about?"

"Well, if you can wait a few minutes, I think I can improve you." Sammi tilted his head, waiting for Mitchell's answer.

"Improve me?" Mitchell sat up. "This perfection?" His hand waved down his body, then he laughed. "I'll wait. Don't take long." He sat back, stroking his shaft.

Sammi dived into the bathroom. He'd been preparing for this all morning. Unplugging the wax pot, he gathered the strips of cloth and a small pair of scissors and hurried back to the bedroom.

After plugging the pot into the socket behind the night table, Sammi picked up the scissors.

"Now, the first phase of construction." He snipped the scissors in the air and sat beside Mitchell. "You need a trim."

Mitchell stared at the scissors. "You're going to be careful with those, right?"

"Very careful." Sammi leaned over, pushed Mitchell's cock to the side and began to trim the thick patch of dark brown hair. He worked for several minutes, trimming it down to just the right length—close, but not so close that it looked sparse.

"Perfect," Sammi pronounced. He ran his fingers through the short thatch and gave Mitchell a sexy grin.

Mitchell touched his pubes and chuckled as he caught the hungry look in Sammi's eyes. "Turns you on?"

"Oh yes, sir." Sammi turned to the wax pot, dipped a finger in to test the molten wax. It was hot, but not too hot. "Perfect."

"Sammi, what are you going to do with that?" Mitchell's eyes widened.

Sammi held up his finger. "This is for your balls. I want them smooth." He dipped his finger again and, taking one of Mitchell's balls, spread the skin tight.

"Hey, you said you were going to do that with your mouth."

"So I did. Oops." Sammi lowered his mouth to Mitchell. With a slow swipe, he licked Mitchell's balls.

Mitchell groaned. "Damn, babe, you're killing me."

"Too bad." Sammi went back to licking, and Mitchell's sac pulled tight against his balls. When Sammi thought they were perfect, he straightened. Mitchell sighed.

Another quick dip of his finger into the pot. He drew it out, waited for the wax not to drip, then wiped his finger all over one side of the tight sac. He picked up a piece of cloth, laid it over the wax, and gave it a soft rubbing to seat the hair in the wax.

"Ready?" He picked up an edge of the strip.

"Is this going to hurt?" Mitchell asked. His brows were raised as he looked down at the cloth stuck to his balls. Sammi felt his fear, but Mitchell's excitement overpowered it.

"Oh, yes, it's going to be delicious." And with that, Sammi ripped the strip off.

Mitchell screamed and his body arched off the bed. Then, he shuddered. His arousal ramped up, flowing into Sammi. Sammi was right. It was fucking delicious. He wanted more.

Sammi worked in silence. Lathering on the wax, laying down the strip, pressing it in. As his eyes locked with Mitchell's, he tore off the cloth. Mitchell's fists caught the sheets of the bed as he twisted beneath Sammi's ministrations.

Such sweet pain, such sweet agony. And Sammi rode it all with him. Mitchell had found the perfect partner, a man who could anticipate his needs and enjoy giving them and receiving them. Sammi was incredible. Beautiful, giving, and so fucking talented as he meted out the pain that Mitchell had craved for so long.

Another rip brought Mitchell's focus on Sammi.

"That was the last one." Sammi grinned.

"No, don't tell me it's over."

"See." Sammi ran oiled fingers over Mitchell's now-smooth balls.

Mitchell's fingers joined Sammi's as they caressed his sac. Mitchell's cock jerked. Sammi smiled and reached for the lube on the table. Spreading it on his hands, he took Mitchell's cock and began stroking it.

Mitchell's head fell back and his eyes shuttered as he opened himself to Sammi. Their pleasure ramped up as it traveled back and forth between them.

"God, this is so good."

Sammi nodded. "I'm not done. Roll over."

Mitchell obeyed.

Sammi's hands ran down Mitchell's back to his firm ass. Dipping his fingers into the valley, he stroked over Mitchell's backdoor. Mitchell gasped. Sammi dunked his finger into the wax pot and spread the cheeks of Mitchell's ass apart with his other hand.

He painted the crevice with wax. Pressed a strip onto one side, then ripped.

"Fuck!" Mitchell shouted. Sammi felt a wave of ecstasy rise up from Mitchell to hit him.

Sammi prepared the other side. Ripped. Mitchell cried out. Once more left Mitchell trembling and softly calling for Sammi.

"Now, to soothe you." Sammi crawled between Mitchell's legs, parted the valley wide, and lowered his mouth to that sweetest of spots. His tongue flicked out, teasing the tight pink rose of Mitchell's ass.

Mitchell's back arched, his hips pumped, as Sammi clutched his ass and unmercifully licked him until he begged Sammi to stop.

Gasping, Mitchell pressed his cock into the bed. Fuck, he wanted to come, but he'd sensed that Sammi wanted more.

"I know what you want," Mitchell whispered.

Sammi sat back on his heels. "What do I want?"

Mitchell's head turned to face his lover as he climbed to his hands and knees.

"Fuck me, babe."

Sammi's arousal pummeled Mitchell. In all the time they'd been together, Sammi had never asked to fuck him. More than anything, Mitchell wanted Sammi inside him and he'd waited long enough for Sammi to get around to it.

"First, I have to tell you something." Sammi bit his lip.

"Tell me anything, babe."

"I took a blood test. At a free clinic."

Mitchell froze. "Oh God, Sammi, please don't tell me…" Tears welled in Mitchell's eyes.

"No, it's not bad. I'm clean, Mitchell. You said you were clean. So, if we're monogamous, then we don't have to use a condom." Sammi gave Mitchell a shy smile.

"That's great news! I'm so relieved." Mitchell laughed. "Now, fuck me and forget the condom."

Trembling with excitement, Sammi got the lube and painted Mitchell's entry. Sammi hadn't been inside a man in years; he'd always been the receiver. The few times he'd done it had been with a couple of the other boys on the strip, but after he fell in with Donovan, all that had come to an end, so to speak. Donovan's customers wanted to fuck Sammi, not be fucked by Sammi.

Ever since he'd met Mitchell, Sammi had wanted this from him but had never thought he was worthy of it. Never thought Mitchell would let him inside. Mitchell was so strong, so dominant, so incredibly male. Sammi loved him for it, but still he longed to feel his prick deep inside the man he loved.

Now, that fantasy was going to come true. Sammi should have known Mitchell would never deny him. Sammi's lack of self-confidence had kept him from asking.

Sammi leaned forward, guiding his cock to Mitchell's portal. Rubbing it up and down against the tender opening, Sammi opened himself to Mitchell's pleasure.

As it washed over him, Sammi realized Mitchell wanted it as badly as he did.

Sammi smeared the lube in his finger and ringed Mitchell's rose. Mitchell moaned. With a little pressure, Sammi's slim finger slipped inside. Mitchell hissed and pressed back against Sammi. Deepening his penetration, Sammi felt for Mitchell's sweet spot, pressing up against the wall of his tunnel. When Mitchell groaned long and loud, Sammi knew he'd found it.

Mitchell shuddered as Sammi worked it, his finger sliding in an out and pressing against the spot. "Oh God, babe, that feels so good."

Sammi's cock was like a steel rod. All his blood seemed to rush to it, just knowing he was turning Mitchell on.

"Fuck me, babe." Mitchell's voice was so deep, so sexy, so needy, it drove Sammi crazy.

He pulled out his finger and gave his cock a few quick strokes, and guided it to Mitchell's opening. He pushed in, and Mitchell's hole spread open, swallowing the head of Sammi's cock. The feeling was indescribable, and to watch it? Shit, he almost lost his load just watching, it was so fucking erotic.

Mitchell was so warm, so tight, and desire flooded Sammi. He pulled out. Mitchell gasped. Sammi entered him again, just rim-deep. Pulled back. Watched as his own cock speared his lover. As Mitchell would say, Damn.

Sammi shallow-fucked Mitchell, until both their desires super-heated, blended, and crashed over them.

"Fuck me deep and hard!" Mitchell pushed back to impale himself on Sammi's rod.

It was all the encouragement Sammi needed. He plunged in, sinking deep until his body touched Mitchell's body. Both men shuddered. Sammi began pumping, taking long, slow strokes, driving the both of them higher. Clutching Mitchell's hips, he buried himself over and over in Mitchell's tight sweet hole as easily as if he'd always taken it.

Mitchell's soft grunting filled Sammi's ears as he fucked him. Sammi's head fell back; his long bangs fell to the side, exposing the look of rapture on his face. "This is so damn good," he cried. "I want to fuck you until you scream."

Mitchell gathered his thoughts and sent them to Sammi.

Sammi's head jerked back. He raised his hand high and then brought it down on Mitchell's rump with a loud slap.

"Damn!" Mitchell shuddered.

Sammi spanked him again, this time harder. A red imprint of Sammi's hand blossomed on Mitchell's right cheek. Mitchell's back arched and his hands twisted in the sheet. "Do it, babe. You know what I want. Hurt me."

Sammi's hand slapped Mitchell's flank until it burned red, but Mitchell merely cried his encouragement, "Fuck, yeah, babe."

He felt Mitchell's orgasm growing, like water rising against a dam, threatening to spill over and wash everything away. Mitchell was ready, but Sammi needed more from him, needed to know he was the one Mitchell wanted and needed.

"Say you're mine," Sammi gasped, his hips pounding into Mitchell.

"I'm yours," Mitchell growled.

"Are you my bitch?" Sammy leaned forward, his hands holding Mitchell tight to him, Sammi's hips moving with all the speed and power he could muster.

"I'm your bitch. Your bitch to fuck," Mitchell gasped, and dropped down to rest his head on the pillow, his ass still in the air.

Sammi's cock hardened beyond aching. Mitchell had submitted to him. Sammi was the dominant and he loved the way it felt. The power of it flooded him. This was what it felt like to take another man, to make him submit to you, to make him beg you to fuck him.

Sammi thrust forward, pushing Mitchell down even farther. Mitchell's legs spread wider as Sammi dominating him, riding him until Mitchell's dam broke and he shot his load, crying out Sammi's name.

Unrelenting, Sammi drove on. His powerful thighs pushed his cock deeper into Mitchell, who slid to his belly with Sammi riding him all the way down. Their ecstasy climbed to new heights as Sammi didn't hold back and Mitchell gave him everything.

"You own me, Sammi. You own my heart and soul, and now you own my body. I'm your sex slave, babe." Mitchell's raspy voice, filled with need and desire, shook with the power of his words as Sammi fucked him.

Sammi cried out Mitchell's name as he exploded. Frozen in the throes of his orgasm, head thrown back, muscles taut and rigid, Sammi was the picture of ecstasy.

He shot his hot load into Mitchell's tunnel as he lay stretched out beneath Sammi. With each of the five hard spurts, shudders racked their bodies. Then it was over and Sammi collapsed on top of Mitchell, wrapping his arms around his lover.

Exhausted, Sammi kissed Mitchell's sweat-soaked back, nuzzled the nape of his neck. "Mitchell, I love you."

"I love you, too." Mitchell whispered. "Damn, Sammi. If I'd have known it was going to be that good, I would have asked for this sooner."

"Thank you, Mitchell. For everything you've given me. It's more—" Sammi's voice caught in his throat and he buried his face against Mitchell's body, letting his tears fall as they dropped onto Mitchell's back.

"No, you deserve everything and more. And I'm just the man to give it to you." Mitchell shifted to the side and Sammi rolled off him.

They lay side-by-side facing each other, kissing slow and languid, enjoying just being together. Touching, stroking fingertips, played against skin, lips brushed over pebbled nipples, cocks stiffened and pressed against taut bellies.

Mitchell wrapped his arms around Sammi and rolled him on top. Sammi looked down into Mitchell's eyes. Mitchell loved him and Sammi didn't need his power to know that. It was in Mitchell's touch, in his voice, his sighs, the shuttering of his eyelids when Sammi touched him. It was unmistakable; even a blind man could see it.

Sammi deserved Mitchell.

Mitchell kissed him. "Fuck me again, Sammi. This time, I want to watch your face when you take me." Mitchell's heated gaze and the hard, thick lump that pressed into Sammi told him that Mitchell was hungry for more. Sammi grabbed Mitchell's hands and pulled them over Mitchell's head, capturing him. Nothing turned Sammi on more than that look in Mitchell's eyes that said, "Fuck me."

Sammi's chest expanded as his breathing deepened and his muscles tensed in preparation of their lovemaking. "You're mine, Mitchell."

"I'm yours. Forever." Mitchell kissed him, pulling Sammi down until their bodies touched, their desire ignited and love engulfed them.

They were bonded. Body, heart, and soul.

 THE END

Lynn Lorenz

Lynn has been writing all her life, but only recently for publication. She writes a variety of genres besides historicals, including police procedurals, fantasy, paranormal, and contemporary romantic comedy, but enjoys reading suspense and detective stories most of all and wishes more cops would fall in love between their pages.

Born in New Orleans, she has a strong affinity for the South, pralines and po'boys. She's never met food she didn't like, but finds it hard to beat the food she grew up with and constantly craves from N'awlins. Going back occasionally to visit her father who still lives there, her car is often laden with epicurean delights such as Hubig Pies, Barqs in the bottle, Central Groceries' muffalattas and Gambino's pastries.

Graduating with a bachelor's degree in Fine Arts, Lynn is also an artist whose still lifes, life studies, and landscapes are done in acrylic, watercolors, pencil, and pastels. She loves getting away for a week at a time just to paint outdoors.

She has a real job that keeps her busy nine-to-five, but in her spare time she finds it hard to stay away from writing. It keeps her off the streets and out of the bars.

Lynn has two incredible kids, a supportive husband of twenty plus years, and a black lab/Aussie sheep dog mix. She's lived in Katy, Texas, since 1999, where she discovered her love of all things Texan and cowboy, like big hair, boots, and blue jeans. Yeehaw!

Find out more about Lynn by visiting her website: http://www.lynnlorenz.com.

FORGOTTEN SONG
Ally Blue

GEORGINA'S DRAGON
Willa Okati

GRACEFUL SUBMISSION
Melinda Barron

HARD CANDY
Angela Knight, Morgan Hawke and Sheri Gilmore

HEAVEN SENT: HELL & PURGATORY
Jet Mykles

LEASHED: MORE THAN A BARGAIN
Jet Mykles

SHARDS OF THE MIND:
THE TA'E'SHA CHRONICLES, BOOK TWO
Theolyn Boese

SLAVE BOY
Evangeline Anderson

THE ASSIGNMENT
Evangeline Anderson

THE BLACKER THE BERRY
Lena Matthews

THE BROKEN H
J. L. Langley

THE RIVALS: SETTLER'S MINE 1
Mechele Armstrong

THE TIN STAR
J. L. Langley

THEIR ONE AND ONLY
Trista Ann Michaels

TRY A LITTLE TENDERNESS
Roslyn Hardy Holcomb

VETERANS 1: THROUGH THE FIRE
Rachel Bo and Liz Andrews

VETERANS 2: NOTHING TO LOSE
Mechele Armstrong and Bobby Michaels

WHY ME?
Treva Harte

Publisher's Note: The print titles listed above were previously released in e-book format by Loose Id®.

Non-Fiction by ANGELA KNIGHT
PASSIONATE INK: A GUIDE TO WRITING EROTIC ROMANCE

Printed in the United States
215950BV00001B/12/P

9 781596 328204